For Mary Ann Grossmann With best wishes, Marty

Doctor Refurb

D1086742

Marty Essen

ENCANTE
PRESS

Published by:

Encante Press, LLC

Victor, MT

Books@EncantePress.com

SAN: 850-4326

Cover design by Betty Martinez

Publisher's Cataloging-in-Publication data

Names: Essen, Marty, author.

Title: Doctor Refurb / Marty Essen. Description: XXXXXXXXXXX

Identifiers: LCCN: XXXXXXX | ISBN: 978-1-7344303-7-0 (pbk.) | 978-1-7344303-6-3 (e-book)

Subjects: XXXXXXXXXXXXXXXXXXXXXXXXX

Classification: XXXXXXXXXXXXXX | XXXXXXXXXXXX

10 9 8 7 6 5 4 3 2 1

Also by Marty Essen

Cool Creatures, Hot Planet: Exploring the Seven Continents

Endangered Edens: Exploring the Arctic National Wildlife Refuge, Costa Rica, the Everglades, and Puerto Rico

Time Is Irreverent

Time Is Irreverent 2: Jesus Christ, Not Again!

Time Is Irreverent 3: Gone for 16 Seconds

Time Is Irreverent: Ooh, It's a Trilogy! (Books 1-3)

Hits, Heathens, and Hippos: Stories from an Agent, Activist, and Adventurer

Special thanks to:

Deb Essen and Sean Essen for their unflinching suggestions.

Dedicated to the memory of all the indigenous children who died in Christian residential schools in Canada and the United States

Contents

Opening Statement

Chapter 1

Terms and Conditions

I didn't think the voice whispering in my head was real at first.

I'm a surgeon at a hospital in a western Montana town. The COVID-19 pandemic had expanded my hours and duties to where pretty much all I was doing was working, eating, and sleeping—and sometimes not the latter. And to make matters worse, my wife of nine years had divorced me eight months ago, complaining that since we were both in our late thirties and didn't already have the complete family package of one-point-nine kids, a dog, and a big house in the city, she was moving on. *Yeah, moving on to Bob, a MAGA-hat-wearing bad boy she met at the hardware store.*

When I said to her, "At least we have Clarice."

She replied, "That mutt? She barely qualifies as a dog! I was serious when I said I wanted a Labradoodle."

Therefore, when a male voice seemed to come out of nowhere to whisper, "If you ask us, they'll be gum," I thought it was either stress or a strange flashback from watching *Field of Dreams* while high on whatever those orange pills were a fellow pre-med student palmed into my hand back in college.

Besides, who wants to be gum? Still, as I visited patient after

1

patient, the voice repeated under the hiss of my respirator, "If you ask us, they'll be gum."

I shook my head to clear my thoughts. Another unvaccinated patient needed my attention—this one gasping for ivermectin when bleach would have been cheaper and just as effective.

When my double shift ended, I washed my hands and face and staggered into the parking lot, where I collapsed into the front seat of my car. I must have fallen asleep, because the sky looked darker when the voice, no longer whispering, startled me out of what I thought was just a daydream.

"Steven. . . . If you ask us, they'll be gum."

"Who is Steven?" I inquired of the voice. "And why should I give a shit about gum? I have enough to worry about already."

"You are not Steven Westinghouse?"

"No! I'm Doctor Stefan Westin."

"Hold on."

"Oh, great," I muttered to myself. "Not only do I have a strange voice in my head, but now it has put me on hold. Some day this has been."

I debated whether to start my car or just sit there. I opted for sitting and occupied my time by tugging on my nose, ears, and other body parts, wondering if any of them would be the equivalent of pressing nine to be put on the *do not speak in my head list.*

"Doctor Westin?"

"Yes, this is still my head."

"Oh good. I just spoke with my supervisor, and I am indeed in the wrong head. Sorry to bother you. . . . Hey, would you be interested in saving your world?"

"That's quite a leap from suggesting I ask about being gum."

My head went silent for a moment before he replied, "I am sorry. . . . I am new at this job and just learned to speak English one Earth-day ago. Overall, I know ninety-two languages—most of them unknown on your planet—and sometimes it takes me a while to become totally comfortable speaking a new one."

"You're not from Earth?"

"Oh, no. I am not even from your galaxy. I am from a planet called. . . . Well, you could not pronounce it. The closest word in your language would be *Philippines.*"

"Naturally."

"So anyway. Do you want to save your world?"

"Of course. What person wouldn't want their world saved? But you still haven't told me what gum has to do with it."

"Oh, dear. . . . I think I meant to say *come.*"

"'If you ask us, they'll be come?' That still doesn't make any sense. Unless you're spelling the word *c-u-m.* But if that's the case, turning someone into cum doesn't seem like something that would save the world from anything."

"One moment, while I check my training class notes."

I closed my eyes and tried to massage away the headache I felt coming on.

The voice returned. "Oh! I was not supposed to say *gum* or *cum.* I was supposed to say *gone.*"

"If you ask us, they'll be gone?"

"Exactly!"

"Well, that makes a little more sense. At least when you find Steven Westinghouse, you won't confuse him as much as you did me."

"Steven Westinghouse? If I select you instead, I may no longer need to speak with him. Hold on."

I exhaled loudly and drummed my fingers on the dashboard.

"Thank you for your patience," the voice said upon returning. "I spoke with my supervisor again, and she looked up your records and declared that you definitely qualify to save your world."

"My records?"

"Yes—voting records, hat-color records, donation records, that sort of thing."

"As a doctor, I'm already having a hard enough time saving people from themselves. What am I supposed to save the world from?"

"The same thing."

"What do you mean?"

"Your species is killing its own planet."

"I agree with you there, but why do you care?"

"That is what my people do. Observing and assisting planets makes our lives complete."

"So somehow I, an overworked doctor, am going to save the world, with the help of a trainee?"

"I am no longer considered a trainee. I am a full-time planetary consultant, third class."

"What does that mean?"

"Hold on."

"Not again!" I clenched my fists and mimed banging my head against the steering wheel.

The voice returned. "Okay. Sorry about that. I just needed to make sure you were eligible for a memory wipe if necessary."

"You will not wipe my memory!"

"Oh, do not worry. I will only wipe your memory if it is *absolutely* necessary. Now, back to your question. As a full-time planetary consultant, third class, I am authorized to seek fulfillment by adopting and helping a dying planet. For liability reasons, a representative of that planet—in this case, you—is necessary to assist me with that experience. Naturally, both of us will have rules to follow. I will get to yours later, but basically mine are that I am solely responsible for the planet I adopt, as well as the planetary representative I select."

"But why me and not Steven Westinghouse? You seem to be pretty lax in your selection process."

"I agree that would be a concern if your planet had a higher ranking. But since Earth is a lesser planet, and this is my first adoption experience, I am allowed some flexibility. You are not wearing a red baseball cap, you do not belong to any cult, you do not vote against the environment, and your profile shows immense caring for others. That is all I require. However, if you want, I can wipe our conversation from your memory and try to locate Steven Westinghouse. I have to warn you, though, that intergalactic memory wipes are not always precise, and since I have never attempted one on an Earth-human before, I cannot guarantee you will not have to go back to medical school and start over."

"I said no memory wipes! Tell me how this works and what I have to do."

"In adopting and nurturing numerous worlds over millions of Earth-years, my people have discovered that the downfall of most planets can be traced to a limited number of influential individuals, and in every such situation, greed and an insatiable desire for power motivated those individuals. All you have to do is ask and they'll be gone."

"Be gone?"

"Oh, it is no big deal. I will not kill them or anything. I will just place an order to have them deported to a depository planet, where they can live out their lives with other beings of similar values."

"What if the people who contributed to the downfall are no longer alive?"

"My training suggested you would ask that. Knowing that I can occupy your brain, you should not have any trouble believing that my species is capable of reaching back in time to grab whomever you name on the date you choose." His voice sped up and grew softer as he added, *"Some-limitations-may-apply."*

"Can I talk this over with my girlfriend and think about it?"

"Sure. You can have two days to do so. And you are in luck! Our updated terms and conditions allow you to choose a single person for both your initial and ongoing consultations. I will enter your girlfriend as that chosen person. Please inform her that she must not discuss our project with anyone other than you. If she does, I will have to give her a deep, ten-year wipe and do the same for anyone she told. Also, if I have to wipe your memory, I must wipe hers too."

"Is there anything else in the terms and conditions I should know?"

"Oh, it is just standard boilerplate stuff. Most beings in similar situations sign their acceptance of the terms and conditions without even bothering to read them. The secrecy and sacrifice clauses are really the only things to be concerned about."

"There's a sacrifice clause?"

"Well, yeah. We cannot have you sending people to the depository planet who do not truly deserve it. To keep you from going all crazy with your new power, our customer service department requires the sacrifice of one body part for each deportation. But do not worry, the process will be quick—to minimize pain—and I will stimulate your body to regrow whatever they extracted."

"No fucking way!"

"Okay. That is totally your choice. Sorry to waste your time, Doctor Westin. I will now commence a memory wipe."

"Wait!"

Chapter 2

Don't Even Say It!

I took a deep breath and held it as I tried to remember the first patient I saw that morning. When that person's name came to me, I exhaled, satisfied that my memory was still intact. "You said I could have two days to decide."

"Do you still want that?" the voice asked.

"Apparently I'm fucked either way. So I might as well use that time to decide which orifice to take it in."

"Okay. Shall we go see your girlfriend?"

"*We?*"

"Well, what do you expect me to do?"

"Leave."

"That is highly unusual, but I suppose it is okay. I will use that time to become more familiar with your language and your planet. Just shout out my name when you have made your decision. I will return in an instant. In the meantime, I will send a customer satisfaction survey to your brain, and you can let me know how I am doing so far. Goodbye for now."

"Wait!"

"Yes?"

"I don't know your name."

"Oh, forgive me. We should have established that a long time ago. Do you prefer a male or a female voice?"

"I have a choice?"

"Of course. That is part of my planet-saving service. Right now, I am using the basic male American Rodney voice. If you prefer something with more character, I can switch to an Australian accent and use the Steve voice—*'Isn't she a beauty!'* Or for something from the north, I can do a Canadian Doug—*'Take off, eh?'* I can also mimic the female voices Siri, Alexa, and Olga."

"Olga?"

"I told you to make a legal U-turn, asshole! Now we're gonna have to drive five miles out of our way! Can't you do anything right?"

"Ah . . . let's just stick with Rodney."

"As you wish."

* * *

Once I was alone, I started my car and took the long way home, via the liquor store. My home is a multiroom log cabin located a few miles outside of town that I purchased after my marriage fell apart. Other than well water that smells of sulfur, it's the perfect place for a recovering divorcé to live. Inside, it features a mostly open floor plan and old but serviceable furniture that was included in my purchase. Outside, it features a large yard and sixteen wooded acres that abut U.S. Forest Service land. I enjoy the privacy, and Clarice, my Labrador-retriever-and-who-knows-what, is thrilled to live where she has lots of room to run and plenty of squirrels to chase.

Shortly after I moved in, the COVID-19 pandemic exploded, forcing me to scramble to find someone to take Clarice outside when I got stuck working late. I solved that problem by paying a bonus to a dog-walking service that agreed to travel a little out of its territory to do the job. It didn't hurt that the proprietor, Tara Kramer, of Tara's Dog Trekkers & Pet Supplies, thought I was cute and took on the job herself rather than farm it out to one of her employees.

Before long, the athletic, sassy brunette was also stopping by the cabin while I was there, offering to take Clarice on a no-charge walk if I was too tired. "It's the least I can do for one of the heroes of the pandemic," she would declare whenever I resisted.

Inevitably, no matter how exhausted I felt, Tara's enthusiasm and the way her big brown eyes looked at me from beneath her bangs always gave me the energy to join in the walk.

My post-divorce resistance to an intimate relationship crumbled a few weeks after those walks began, and I asked her out on a date. From there, our relationship moved quickly, as she took over three-quarters of my tiny closet and began spending her nights with Clarice and me.

While I'm not yet ready to jump into another marriage, Tara and I are now serious enough to consider ourselves exclusive. She's also the person I know I can trust to keep my secret and to provide levelheaded advice.

* * *

"Are you fucking insane?" Tara shrieked after I recapped my conversation with Rodney.

We were sitting on my dilapidated couch, in what passed for the cabin's living room, with stiff drinks in hand, and Clarice between us—lobbying for us to take her on a walk.

"I know it sounds insane, but I didn't imagine it. Think of the good I—let's make that *we*—could do? We'd have to make a list. But what if we could get rid of Hitler before he rose to power? And I can think of a handful of current politicians the world would be better off without, too."

She looked at me and tilted her head. "Stefan, if this is some sick practical joke, I swear I will quite literally rip your balls off and feed them to a Rottweiler."

"I'm not joking."

"And if you don't play along with Rodney, he'll wipe your memory?"

"Yes, and since I've told you, if he has to wipe my memory, he'll wipe your memory too. On top of that, you absolutely must tell no one. If you do, he'll wipe your memory plus the memory of anyone you told."

"Do you think he actually has the power to wipe a person's memory?" Tara asked.

"I guess it's possible he's only using that as a threat to get my cooperation. But considering that he's already demonstrated the ability to speak inside my head, I see no reason why wiping someone's memory would be beyond his powers."

"What if you accept but do nothing or only provide him with a list of insignificant people who've already died?"

I sipped my drink before answering, "I didn't ask, but I'm sure the consequences are somewhere in the list of terms and conditions I have to sign."

"You have to sign terms and conditions?"

"Yeah, apparently Rodney is the AT&T of aliens."

"At least there's a bright side. Saving the world is a good thing. Isn't it?"

"Sure, but losing a body part—even if it's only temporary—will be dreadful."

"I can't think of anything more macabre. You don't think he'd cut off your—"

"*Shhh!*" I shuddered. "Don't even say it."

She widened her eyes. "But maybe it would grow back bigger."

"Do you have a problem with my size?"

"No! I'm kidding. I think you're just the right size." She

grinned. "But if he takes your ears, perhaps you can suggest a bit of a tuck when they grow back."

"How about my hair? If he takes it, should I ask him to change it from light brown to black or to add a little curl?"

"No, I like your hair the way it is. And besides, there's little sacrifice in taking your hair. If he did anything like that, he'd take your scalp too."

I swallowed hard and said, "I feel ill."

"We need a plan."

"I agree. And that plan has to start with acquiring some heavy-duty painkillers. Rodney said the removals will be quick, but there will still be pain."

"Then it's a good thing you're a doctor."

"Do you know anything about medicine? Did you take a first aid class in school or anything?"

She scowled at me for a moment before saying, "Don't you remember? I told you on our first date that I have a vet tech degree and worked in a veterinarian's office for three years. I changed careers when caring for sick animals grew too depressing, and the call of the outdoors enticed me to start my dog walking business."

"Sorry. I had the first-date-after-a-divorce-jitters. So much of that night is a blur."

Tara and I sat in silence for a moment, providing Clarice with the only cue she needed to increase her lobbying to another level. We downed the last of our drinks and relented to a walk through the forest. Getting outside for a bit was good for all of us, even if the crisp fall air didn't give me the jolt of energy I had hoped it would. At least Clarice got the exercise she needed, putting on five times the distance the humans did. A contented dog would mean one last distraction for us to deal with.

Upon our return, I built a fire in the woodstove, and Tara and I snuggled up on the couch and tried to develop a plan. Exhaustion soon overcame me, however, and a pot of coffee was out of the question. I had to be back at the hospital by seven in the morning to deal with more unvaccinated patients on ventilators.

"I don't have the energy to move to the bed," I whispered.

"That's okay. It's comfy out here by the fire." She picked up her phone and set the alarm. "Before we agree to anything, we must insist that Rodney meet with us in person to answer all our questions." She turned out the light.

Chapter 3

The Rush Limbaugh Demo

I arrived at the hospital with barely enough coffee in me to hide my exhaustion, yet more than enough to keep me rushing to the bathroom between patients. Montana's COVID-19 cases tended to arrive in waves, and the current one, spurred on by a major right-wing event where no one wore masks, was making me struggle to give each patient the attention he or she deserved.

Well, perhaps *deserved* is the wrong word to use. That's because, at least in my opinion, those who refused vaccinations only to show up later with severe symptoms, demanding quack cures, really didn't deserve the same level of treatment as those who did everything they were supposed to do and still suffered a breakthrough case. And what about those who suffered something unrelated to the pandemic, only to have to transfer elsewhere or wait for a bed to open up?

Even so, I kept to myself the urge to ask those who had refused vaccinations if all the pain they were experiencing was worth it to "own the libs." Yes, even the most obstinate of my patients received the best care I could give them. Who knew that being a COVID-era doctor would require acting talent worthy of an Oscar?

Today, fortunately, I didn't lose any patients. That was something I hadn't celebrated nearly enough in recent weeks. My unusually mundane shift allowed me to contemplate whether I actually had it in me to steal the painkillers necessary to endure what Rodney proposed.

Acquiring opioids, from morphine to fentanyl, would be relatively easy for me. Doctors commonly prescribed larger doses of morphine than their heart attack and other operating room patients needed. What they didn't inject through the cannula remained in the syringe for disposal, and sometimes patients even returned unused medications for disposal. Those acquisitions would be risk-free. Acquiring additional opioids from the hospital pharmacy wouldn't be much more difficult—especially for someone like me, who had been working at the hospital for years and had earned the respect of the staff. I'd just have to be careful to avoid any out-of-the-ordinary requests, and frankly, the COVID-19 pandemic would make drawing attention to my requests virtually impossible.

I finished my shift, slipped some medication into my pocket, said goodbye to a few co-workers, and headed home for the weekend. That Friday had arrived was fortunate. Now I'd have the evening and all day Saturday to catch up on my sleep and make a rational decision about how to handle this new opportunity—or terrible mistake.

* * *

Tara and Clarice were waiting for me when I stepped through the front door of the cabin, which enters into the kitchen.

"Did you—" Tara began.

I waved her off. "All I want is to enjoy a quiet dinner and then bundle up and take a walk through the woods with you and Clarice." I hung my jacket behind the door and plopped into the chair at the kitchen table opposite Tara. "We'll discuss our predicament later. Right now, the last thing I want to think about is anything that has to do with Rodney!"

"Hi, Stefan!" Rodney blurted into my brain. "Are you ready to proceed?"

"Proceed? We agreed that I'd shout out your name when I made my decision."

"Isn't that what you just did?"

"That wasn't a shout-out."

"It sure sounded like one to me."

"No, it—" I stopped when Tara shot me an inquisitive half-smile. "Hold on." I returned her smile and tapped my finger on the side of my head. "It's Rodney," I whispered.

"Yeah, I kinda figured that out. Tell him Tara says hi."

"Rodney?"

"Yes."

"Tara says hi."

"Is Tara the girlfriend you wish to consult with—subject to the secrecy clause in the terms and conditions?"

"You haven't shown me the terms and conditions!"

"That is okay. Her knowing about me automatically binds her to those terms and conditions. Now when you are ready to sign your own copy, we will not need to have Tara do the same. That will save us a lot of time! Isn't that wonderful?"

"Oh, yeah," I replied with all the sarcasm I could muster. "Just wonderful."

"What did he say?" Tara asked.

I looked at her and said, "This is gonna get confusing." I

glanced toward the ceiling and said, "Rodney, since you claim Tara is now contractually part of this, you need to let her hear you."

"I also want to see him," she added.

"She wants to see you, too."

"I am not sure if . . . Hold on."

I grinned at Tara. "He put me on hold to check with his supervisor."

She grinned back. "Do you want me to mix us some cocktails while we wait?"

"Oh, yeah," I replied with all the appreciation I could muster. "That would be wonderful."

We were taking the first sips of our drinks when Rodney returned.

"I have good news and bad news," he said.

I looked up and asked, "What's the bad news?"

"Ever since a certain unfortunate incident that my supervisor will not let me discuss with you at this time, my people have been forbidden from physically traveling to your planet. Sorry. An in-person visit is out of the question."

"What's the good news?"

"The good news is that I was able to get permission to activate conference-occupying with visual mode. Are you ready?"

"Let me inform Tara, so the surprise doesn't make her spill her drink." I looked down and said, "Rodney isn't allowed to set foot on Earth, but he got permission to conference us all in using visual mode. I don't know what that will be like, but I'm guessing he's gonna appear inside our heads. Brace yourself."

I looked back up. "Okay, Rodney. We're ready to see you now."

"Ta-da!" he exclaimed.

"Trevor Noah!" Tara blurted.

Rodney had appeared inside our brains as if he were in front of a green screen. Wherever we looked, there he was in the foreground, wearing a blue hoodie. I can't say if he was projecting an image into our brains or reaching us like a vivid dream, but I could have sworn he was directly inside my head, which had become a cavernous, well-lit theater.

"So, what do you think?" he asked.

"You are not Trevor Noah," I said.

"I know. But an actual image of me presented in this manner would blow out your occipital lobe. My research shows that you both watch *The Daily Show,* so I thought using Trevor Noah as my avatar would be comforting for you. If you want, I can take the form of someone else. Rowan Atkinson perhaps?"

"Actually Rowan would be . . . never mind," I said.

"Okay, Trevor Noah it is."

"But can you sync your voice with your lips?" Tara asked. "Your voice is slightly behind them, and it's really distracting."

"Sorry, that is a known bug that tech support has been working on for thousands of years. They cannot seem to fix it."

"How about your voice?" I asked. "It's even more distracting hearing the basic male American voice coming out of that face."

"Hold on."

He disappeared for a moment before returning. "Okay. How do I sound now?"

"What do you call an animal that looks like a horse with stripes?" I asked.

"A *zeb-bra.*"

"Perfect."

"Would you like to call me Trevor, too?"

"Absolutely not," I said. "You're most definitely a Rodney."

Tara looked up. "Hey, Rodney. It's nice to meet you and all, but aside from this kind of freaking me out, Stefan and I really need some time to discuss our situation. Also, I know Stefan will be a lot more productive once he's had a good night's sleep. Can you give us some more time? We'll shout out for you on Sunday."

"Sure, I will give you until then, if you will allow me to present you with a short demonstration before I leave."

"I guess that's agreeable," I said.

"Oh, good! In the future, I may make suggestions on whom we send to the depository planet, but the ultimate decision will always be up to you. This time, however, I went ahead and selected someone universally accepted as an environmental villain: Rush Limbaugh. Let me demonstrate the benefits of deporting him."

"He's already dead," Tara said.

"But when did he die? Look it up on whatever website you like."

I grabbed my laptop from beside the couch and carried it over to the kitchen table. "His Wikipedia page says February 17, 2021."

"Are you sure?" Rodney asked. "Wikipedia is not always accurate. Check some other sources."

I entered a search and clicked on several pages. "Yep. They all say February 17th."

"That is too long on Earth for someone like him. What do you say we shorten his life by a week?"

"Oh . . . kay," I said hesitantly.

He blinked out for a second before returning and dramatically flicking out his right arm. "Ta-da! My supervisor has confirmed your order. On February 10, our transfer division removed Limbaugh's living body from Earth. It is now at our transfer facility and will soon be on its way to the depository planet. On that same date, the transfer division also replaced Limbaugh's body with an inanimate replica, suitable for Earth's burial rituals. Look at those same web pages now."

I refreshed the pages. "They all say February 10, 2021."

He flashed a smile. "Was that fun?"

"Um . . . Kind of," I said.

"And now, your sacrifice." He flicked out his arm again.

My right foot exploded in white-hot pain! I fell to the floor, screaming, *"Ahhh! Shiiit!"*

"It was just the nail on your big toe," he said calmly. "It will grow back."

"Do you . . . know how . . . much it hurts . . . to have a toenail ripped off?" I asked between gasps.

"Not really. I have never had a use for nails of any kind." He held my toenail in front of his eyes to examine it.

"Wait! You have my toenail?"

"Isn't that the point of a sacrifice?"

"You're sick!"

"Perhaps . . . from your point of view. From my point of view, I am just maintaining the balance of good and bad. Cutting Rush Limbaugh's life on Earth by a week removed only a little of the bad. That is why your sacrifice to replace the bad was so small."

I took a few deep breaths to help dissipate the pain before continuing. "I would argue that removing Limbaugh actually added more good to the balance. At that point in his life, Limbaugh was no longer on the air to spread lies and hate, and dying of lung cancer is a terrible way to go. So, in reality, all you did was eliminate a week of his suffering—at least his suffering on Earth. Therefore, if you have the capability to do so, you must reattach my toenail."

"Hold on." He disappeared.

Tara helped me onto my chair before hurrying to the bathroom for a bandage and some disinfectant. As she stepped back into the kitchen, Rodney reappeared in our heads.

"My supervisor appreciates your thoughtfulness and has approved a toenail return. Also, since we caused you unnecessary pain, I am authorized to credit your account for an additional free Rapid Return Body Part to be redeemed within the next thirty days." His voice sped up and grew softer as he said, "Offer-good-on-Planet-Earth-only-Rapid-Return-Body-Parts-will-be-refur-bished-substitutes-of-similar-appearance-Please-use-responsi-bly-Some-limitations-may-apply." Then, after a brief pause, he flicked out his arm and shouted, "Ta-da!"

My pain melted away. Then I focused on Rodney's right hand. "My toe feels much better, but you're still holding my nail."

"That is because of our Rapid Return Body Part Service. Returning your original body part is quite difficult and highly inefficient. Therefore, your new toenail is a refurbished model."

I yanked off my shoe and sock and stared at my toe. The nail was back, but it was shinier than the others and longer too. I was a doctor, and therefore used to seeing transplants. Tara, on the other hand, looked down at my foot, gasped, and made a run for the bathroom.

"Rodney, get out of my head!" she screamed. "I need some privacy."

I had no way of knowing if Rodney actually left Tara's head, but the way he shuffled from one side of my head to the other, as if he were a man at a quilt show pretending to be interested in what he saw, made me assume his full attention was on me.

"Just looking around," he finally whispered. "Your hippocampus appears to be quite healthy."

When I heard the toilet flush and Tara's footsteps, Rodney hurried to a position that at least presented the illusion of him being directly behind my eyes. He smiled. "Oh, good. She is back."

Tara lost her balance for a moment, only to regain it by grab-bing the edge of the kitchen table. "Hey, Rodney," she said. "Can you at least give me some sort of warning before popping in like that? If you suddenly interfere with half my vision at the wrong time, you could cause a nasty accident."

"I will knock next time," he said.

"Can we please break for the weekend now?" I asked.

"Since you have experienced the demonstration, I will abide by my part of our agreement and leave you alone. But before I go, Stefan, I want to remind you that you qualified to save your world because of your caring personality. Although I cannot see into the future, my people have observed enough planetary extinctions to know Earth is headed for disaster without a course correction. If you do nothing, a memory wipe will be the least of your problems. Extreme climate change will lead to civil wars, nuclear wars, dramatic losses of human rights, and viruses that you will wish were only as bad as COVID-19. Some of those events will happen in your lifetime; others will happen a few generations further into the future. But no matter what, most life on your planet will face extinction within two hundred years."

I swirled what was left of my drink and asked, "If you know what needs to be done, why involve me or anyone else? Why not just fix it yourself?"

"I cannot do so, because my people work in mysterious ways."

I slammed my glass on the table. "Oh, bullshit, Rodney! What's the real reason?"

"Hold—"

"No! I won't hold on. Either you tell me right now or connect me with your supervisor."

"Great idea!" Tara added. "And I bet this conversation is being recorded for quality and training purposes."

Rodney pushed out his hands. *"Shhh!* Okay, the real reason we have decided to work through a human is that we tried direct intervention on your planet in the past. It failed. That failure led to the travel ban to your planet. My people do not deal well with failure. But this time, if you make the decisions and serve as our earthbound agent—no matter how much I guide you—my superiors will not have to accept any responsibility. Unless, of course, you are successful. Then they will bask in the glory of saving

Earth from devastation. Your success will also mean a nice promotion for me!"

I rolled my eyes. "Well, thanks for the honesty. . . . I think."

"I will be off now," he said. "Enjoy your new toenail. The refurbished version is enhanced. You can drop a brick on the thing and it will not crack."

"I'll take your word for it."

Chapter 4

Superhero

Tara and I sat quietly at the kitchen table until we were sure Rodney had departed. She moved first, carrying our glasses to the counter and refilling them. As she handed me a fresh drink she said, "I thought having you as a boyfriend would add stability to my life."

"I haven't yet decided to accept Rodney's offer."

She slid back into her chair and said, "Of course you're going to accept it. Neither of us knows how much damage an alien memory wipe could do to a brain. You could lose your job; I might forget I had one; we could become strangers; . . . and the list goes on. Besides, who better than us to handle this responsibility? Sure, it's sick, but we might be able to make the world a lot less sick than the next person he'd choose. Also, your medical experience and access to painkillers, plus my medical experience, will help you survive."

"I'm not sure I want to be treated by a vet tech."

"Oh, come on! I took a class in primate biology. It's not as if I'll need to cure you of cancer."

"I'm surprised you're willing to go along with this."

"Like I said, if not us, who? Besides, I agree with Rodney that our planet is in real trouble. We just might be able to fix that."

"All while I get sliced and diced and possibly addicted to painkillers."

She reached across the table and squeezed my hand. "Do you want me to ask if I can take your place?"

"No!"

"Then shut up and be a hero."

"You know, some people already think I'm a hero."

"Oh, there's no doubt about that—just like everyone else in the medical profession who deals with COVID-19 patients day after day. But now you can be a superhero."

I raised my glass. "Just call me Doctor Refurb."

* * *

I awoke the next morning after the best night's sleep I'd had in weeks. By all rights, I should have tossed and turned all night. I guess it was just a strange combination of exhaustion and anticipation. I went into medicine to help people, and over the years, I had helped more than a thousand. Now I could help an entire planet.

My primary concern was how I would deal with the ethics of deporting someone—no matter how horrible that person was. And while Rodney's claim that he would send people I selected to a depository planet, not kill them, eased the moral dilemma of it all, I had no way of knowing if he was being truthful.

My other worry was whether I was qualified to judge others. That worry was fairly easy to discount, however, because in the United States we had juries that routinely refused to convict cops for beating and killing blacks, judges who let the rich off for crimes that would send a poor person to prison, and two Supreme Court justices who had likely assaulted women. If society deemed those individuals suitable to judge, I was more than qualified for the task. On top of that, Tara would be beside me to provide a second opinion, should I make an error in judgement.

Her words from the previous night echoed in my brain: "If not us, who?"

I took a shower before padding into the kitchen, where Tara had a pot of coffee perking and eggs crackling on the stove.

"Good morning, Doctor Refurb!" she said with a grin.

"Oh, God. I knew I was gonna regret coming up with that moniker as soon as I said it. Is that what you're going to call me from now on? It was only a toenail."

"So far."

I settled into my usual chair and said, "Rodney promised to stimulate regrowth of whatever he takes."

"We'll see about that. He's obviously not going to take anything that would kill you. Otherwise, his project would end. Still, I doubt his species has a toenail fetish. Didn't you tell me that the first time he spoke with you, he declared that the purpose of the body part extractions was to keep you from going overboard with your power and sending people who didn't deserve it to the depository planet?"

"Yes."

"In that case, I'm pretty sure you can count on him upping the penalty as time goes on. Imagine if he took your heart or lungs. You'd die unless they were immediately replaced with refurbished organs."

"Do I have to imagine that?"

She smiled. "I just want you to know that my calling you Doctor Refurb is likely gonna stick around for a while."

"Swell."

* * *

Tara and I spent most of Saturday inside the cabin, only stepping outside for occasional walks with Clarice. During that time, we compiled a list of people—both past and present—who we thought were most devastating to life on Earth.

Looking at that list afterward, I realized that most of the people on it were Americans. Surely America didn't have a monopoly on the greedy, the evil, and the dangerous.

Yet one thing I learned while traveling overseas for a medical conference was that people outside the United States knew far more about the lives of Americans than Americans knew about the lives of people overseas. I returned from that trip vowing to pay better attention to what happened in other countries. Now I realized I hadn't lived up to that vow and didn't have time to correct it. All I could do was recognize my failure as we moved forward and jot down a note to ask Rodney for his assistance in selecting people who lived outside the U.S.

Also on our list was what to do with our jobs. Tara was lucky enough to have three reliable employees who would be eager to pick up some extra hours in the event she had to take care of me for an extended period.

My situation was a little more tricky. Although I had some vacation time coming, taking a vacation during a pandemic would not only be totally out of character for me, it would be irresponsible too. On the other hand, I couldn't very well show up at work with a missing foot and say, "Oh, it's no big deal. It'll grow back."

And if I was going to be gone from work, how would I get the necessary painkillers? Surely what I grabbed earlier wouldn't be enough. Ultimately, we decided that I would return to the hospital before the weekend was over to acquire some more drugs.

Before traveling there, however, the two of us sat facing each other on the couch and debated whom to target for the initial round of "If you ask us, they'll be gone."

"Adolf Hitler," Tara suggested.

"What about going back in time and deporting Donald Trump when he was still a game show host?" I asked. "Aside from treating climate change as a hoax, he was also the person most responsible for the rapid spread of the COVID-19 pandemic in America. With him gone, the pandemic will still exist, but the numbers of sick and dead will be much smaller. That move alone could eliminate hospital overcrowding and save well over two hundred thousand lives."

"Both need to go, but I think you'll feel better about yourself if you deport Hitler first. As vile as Trump is, he's still a living person, and the morality of deporting him may haunt you. But Hitler? There's no question his deportation will put you way ahead in the morality versus evilness game I know you'll play in your head from the very start."

"I suppose it might be better to begin with someone from the past to see how everything unfolds, too."

"Exactly!"

* * *

Having settled on an initial deportee, we concluded our Saturday with a late-night trip to the hospital, where Tara served as a lookout while I grabbed more painkillers.

I left a voice mail message for my head nurse as we rode home: "Hi, Sharon. Earlier today, I started feeling under the weather. I stopped by my office to give myself a COVID-19 quick test. Wouldn't you know, it came back positive. I guess I shouldn't have waited to get that booster shot. Anyway, my symptoms are minor. I'll let you know if they worsen and will be quarantining at my cabin until further notice."

When Sunday morning arrived, we stayed in bed late, though not entirely for sleep.

"Hey," said Tara. "If Rodney takes your penis, this may be the last time we get to use it for a while. Let's make the most of it."

"He's not going to take my penis!" I insisted. Nevertheless, now that she had put that thought out there for all to hear, said penis had trouble thinking of anything else and was just a wee bit reluctant to join in the fun.

Shortly after lunch, I called out from the kitchen table, "Rodney, are you there?"

Chapter 5

The Creeps

Rodney materialized, wearing a bright smile. "Are you ready to save your planet?"

"As ready as I'll ever be," I said. "I just have a few more questions."

He clasped his hands behind his back and began rocking on his heels. "Go ahead."

"Do I have a choice in the body parts you take?"

"No. My supervisor makes that decision."

"Do you ever take the same body part more than once?"

"No. Rotating through the parts keeps things more interesting."

I glanced at the note pad on the table and tapped the next question with my pen. "As Tara and I compiled a list of deportation candidates, I realized our knowledge of people in other countries was lacking and was relieved when I remembered your offer to make deportation suggestions. But if you are just learning about life on Earth, how can either of us trust that your suggestions will be any better than ours?"

He nodded. "That is part of my job as a full-time planetary

consultant, third class. I can absorb more information in five Earth-minutes than most humans can absorb in a lifetime. And even though I cannot see into the future, I also have a number of highly advanced prediction tools at my disposal. Most importantly, since eliminating people in the past will change the future, I will run multiple simulations beforehand to make sure you are not doing more harm than good. Imagine if you unwittingly eliminated a distant relative that would cause you not to be born. This project would end in a hurry, and your planet would be doomed."

"I hadn't thought about that. You must promise me that you'll run the same simulations for Tara. We're a team. If she disappears, you might as well just wipe my memory because the pain of what we did would be too great. I wouldn't be able to continue."

"Oh, you're so sweet, Stefan," Tara said.

"I agree," said Rodney.

"You agree that I'm sweet, or you agree to my terms?" I asked.

"I agree to your terms. But as I said, I cannot see into the future. I can only run simulations to predict it."

"Have you ever lost someone that way before?" Tara asked.

"Perhaps Stefan did not tell you. This is my first planet-saving assignment. Therefore, I can honestly say that I have never lost a single person."

"What about others of your kind who have similar jobs, involving other planets?" Tara asked.

"I do not think any species, no matter how advanced, is perfect all the time. Here, however, if either of you disappeared, it would almost certainly be because of human error."

"Human error?" she asked.

"Yes. All I can do is rapidly search birth records. If a record is missing, or if a biological parent is misidentified, there is always a chance I could deport an unknown ancestor of yours."

"Can you reverse a mistake?" I asked.

"That depends."

"Depends on what?"

"How quickly I can reach a supervisor in the transfer division. Once someone arrives at the depository planet, we permanently block that person's retrieval. If we did not do that, the people we send there would eventually figure out how to return to their home planets, and we would have deportees rising from the dead all over the place."

"Are your supervisors as hard to get ahold of as Amazon's are?" Tara asked.

He shook his head. "Oh, please! We are an advanced species."

Tara stared out the kitchen window, and I stroked Clarice's back, neither of us sure what to ask next.

Rodney allowed us only a moment of silence before continuing. "Okay, if neither of you has any more questions, I propose we get started right away. Stefan, I recommend that you move to someplace comfortable and perhaps sit on some plastic."

My stomach churned. "Plastic? Are you saying there will be blood? Should Tara have some suture ready?"

"Do not worry about that. Closing the wound is one of my many jobs. Depending on what my supervisor asks the customer service department to extract, you might experience some brief splattering. That is all."

I stood, but before I could take a step, wooziness overcame me. Several deep breaths helped me recover just enough to run to the bathroom and vomit. Apparently, I wasn't as brave as I had convinced myself I would be.

When I returned, Tara had a couch cushion lined with a large, ripped-open plastic garbage bag. The plastic crackled as I sat next to her. She leaned over and kissed me.

Once Rodney felt we were sufficiently situated, he clasped his hands in front of his chin and said, "So! Have you thought about whom you want to deport first?"

"Yes," I said. "Adolf Hitler."

"I am afraid not."

"Why?"

"Normally, after you suggest someone, I will run a simulation. Hitler, however, was such an obvious choice that I ran the simulation ahead of time. He was a horrible human being and all, but my people are unconcerned with that. What we are concerned about is the long-term viability of your planet. Deporting Hitler projects as providing practically no environmental benefits. Sorry. He stays."

"But wasn't starting a World War and gassing the Jews detrimental to the environment?"

"Yes."

"Then I want to deport Hitler."

"Hold on." He vanished.

I made eye contact with Tara and shook my head as we waited.

Rodney popped back a moment later. "My supervisor said no, but you are welcome to file an appeal to her supervisor."

"How do I do that?"

"A form will appear in your brain momentarily. Just mentally click the box beside the paragraph listing the reason for your appeal and accept the terms and conditions. You will be notified of a decision in three to six weeks."

I waited for the form to arrive, clicked the necessary boxes, and watched the form disappear.

"Your next selection, please."

"That's it?" I asked.

"Yes," he said. "Next."

"Okay. How 'bout Donald Trump?"

"Ooh! That is a big decision. The deportation of the living president of the most powerful nation on your planet fits in our largest sacrifice category. Are you sure you do not want to start smaller?"

"Perhaps you haven't heard. Donald Trump is no longer the president of the United States."

Rodney wagged a finger back and forth, as he replied in a singsongy voice, "That is not what some people say."

"Stefan, wait," Tara said. "I have a better idea: Fred Trump."

"Donald's father?" I asked.

"Yes! If we eliminate Fred before he reproduces, not only does Donald Trump Senior never exist, but neither do his children. Donald Trump Junior gives me the creeps!"

I broke into a smile. "And from what I've read about Fred Trump, it's easy to understand how Donald Senior turned out the way he did. What do ya say, Rodney? We could deport Fred just before he fathers his first child. Since he was never a political leader, he shouldn't require as big of a sacrifice either."

"Hold on while I run some simulations." He disappeared.

With my brain temporarily unoccupied, I took Clarice outside for what very well could be the last pee break I'd be able to accompany her on for quite some time.

When I returned, Tara was still on the couch—now holding my laptop computer. Rodney reappeared the moment I joined her.

"I have good news and bad news," he said, as he began to pace. "The good news is that neither you nor Tara will cease to exist, and with Donald Trump out of the picture, Hillary Clinton will almost certainly become America's first female president. As a result, Trump's damage to the environment will instantly vanish and be replaced by Clinton's modest environmental progress. Also, her more competent handling of the COVID-19 pandemic will likely save hundreds of thousands of lives. The bad news is that despite all that, most projections show Clinton failing to be reelected and the president who follows her failing to continue the environmental policies enacted under her."

"How accurate are your projections?" I asked.

"Every world is different, but all planetary consultants strive for accuracy in the 93 to 96 percent range. Anything less and we would not be deserving of our jobs."

"I can live with that."

"Me too," echoed Tara.

"I also ran a separate long-range simulation to make sure your selection would actually improve the chance of survival for life on your planet. After all, we cannot just deport someone because they give you the creeps or you disagree with their politics. In this instance, I needed to examine everyone who would disappear, not just Fred and Donald Senior. For example, what if Donald Junior was destined to become president and behave exactly the opposite of his father and lead a pro-environment revolution?"

Tara burst into laughter and said, "I don't think you need to worry about that."

"You are correct. My simulator actually came back with a sarcastic response that essentially said, 'Are you fucking kidding me?' Other than a rebellious niece, significant positive contributions to humanity from the Trump family are rare, and no one projects as doing anything to extend the longevity of life on your planet."

"Oh. I hadn't considered Mary Trump," I said. "She seems to be a good person."

Rodney stopped his pacing to add an illusion to his repertoire. He reached through the side of my head, pulled in a virtual chair, unfolded it, sat, and leaned forward before quietly saying, "You have a real moral dilemma. The pain of losing a body part is temporary; the pain of eliminating innocent lives sticks with you forever. Unfortunately, the further you go back in time to eliminate someone, the more innocent lives you affect. For that reason, I discourage going back any further than the beginning of the twentieth century. Earlier than that, the question of whether you are doing your planet any good becomes too unpredictable. With that in mind, all I can say is that deporting Fred Trump before he reproduces projects as being both timeline safe and biologically less expensive than directly deporting his president son. Whether it is worth eliminating Mary Trump is a decision only you can make."

"What if we deported Donald Trump while he was still in the womb?" I asked.

"Similar womb deportation questions come up frequently on other planets, so that was something covered extensively in my training," Rodney said. "As an advanced species, my people take the stand that a fetus is part of a woman's body, and whether to keep it or remove it is her decision alone. Therefore, if we deported the fetus, we would immediately have to stimulate the woman's body to rapidly regrow a new one or replace it with a refurb. Either way, since parenting plays such an important role in human development, it is highly unlikely that an in-womb switch would accomplish the desired result."

"Can we just deport Fred Trump's penis before he impregnates Mary Anne with Donald?" Tara asked.

I chuckled and said, "Great idea!"

Rodney frowned. "I am sorry, but the refurb/regrow dilemma still applies. A penis is part of Fred's body, and whether to keep it or remove it is his decision alone. A refurbished unit would be instantly usable, and even though a regrow procedure would certainly halt Fred's sex life for a while, the fact that he would ultimately regrow his penis would become huge national news. Donald Trump's supporters already treat him as a demigod. Imagine his status if he were the first person spawned from a regrown penis?"

"Did Fred Trump have any children after Donald?" I asked.

Tara opened a webpage that displayed the Trump family tree and tilted the laptop screen so I could see what she was looking at.

"Yes," she said, "Robert Trump. But he didn't have any biological children."

"Then I've got it," I said. "We'll deport Fred Trump in early 1945, before the sex act that spawned Donald. That'll save the lives of Mary and others in the Trump family, who will have little or no effect on the decline of our planet."

"Is that your final decision?" Rodney asked.

"Yes."

He closed his eyes. "I am just running one last simulation and waiting for my supervisor's approval."

He opened his eyes. "Excellent. My supervisor has given the deportation her blessing, and despite Republicans later reversing most of President Hillary Clinton's environmental programs, simulations still show significant progress toward saving your planet. I am sending a deportation agreement to your brain. Just initial the terms and conditions and sign at the bottom."

"Can I read the agreement first?"

"The document is quite long, and it contains legalese that would make even the best attorney on Earth weep with jealousy. But by all means, read as much as you like."

I squinted my eyes out of habit and began. After three pages, I skimmed and scrolled. Finally, I gave up and moved to the end of the document, where I initialed and signed.

"Okay," said Rodney. "This is the moment we have all been waiting for. Just nod, and we will get started."

I nodded.

Chapter 6

Raising the Dead

B lood splattered on the far wall!
I screamed in pain! "Oh, fuck! You took my leg! Fu—"
I passed out.

When I awoke, an hour or so later, Tara had the stump of my left leg bandaged and a shot of morphine in my arm. I watched her clean up around me until my mind felt unclouded enough to speak. Then I said in a slow, throaty voice, "Rodney, you fucking sick bastard. You led me to believe Fred Trump would cost me something small, like a finger or a toe, not something major, like a leg."

He materialized, wearing a concerned expression. "I am very sorry. I told you I was a full-time planetary consultant, third class. At that rank, all I can do is recommend candidates for deportation and suggest appropriate sacrifices and let my supervisor take it from there. Once I reach first class, I will have full control over everything."

"How long will it take for my leg to grow back?"

"Not long. Perhaps two or three months."

I sighed.

My cell phone pinged from the kitchen table, indicating a text message had arrived.

I looked at Tara and said, "The only people who have my private number are you and the hospital, and they would only bother me on a Sunday if it was an emergency. Can you check for me? I don't seem to be able to walk at the moment."

She stepped over to the table and looked at the screen. "It's from someone named Amy."

"My sister? That's impossible! Didn't I tell you she was a nurse, who died when the first COVID-19 wave hit Mont—" I froze.

"—ana," finished Tara. "Amy says, 'Hi Bro! I'll be there in five minutes. Bringing wine.'"

I shouted in a panic, "Rodney! What do I do? Can you add my sister to the list of people who know what's going on? Obviously, I can't hide a missing leg!"

He shook his head. "I am sorry. The terms and conditions only allow for one person to give you guidance, and you have already selected Tara. If Amy finds out, I will have no choice but to wipe her memory."

I grimaced. "Shit! There must be something you can do."

"You have a credit on your account for one free Rapid Body Part Return. Would you like to use that now?"

"Yes!"

"Hold on."

A new leg attached itself to me within seconds.

"Ta-da!" Rodney shouted.

Tara had stripped me to my underwear after I passed out, so it took only an instant to realize something was very wrong. "Rodney! What did you give me? Kobe Bryant's leg?"

"Oh, dear," he said.

At least the pain was gone. I did my best to stand, but it was difficult, since the right leg I was born with matched my six-foot height and my new left leg matched someone a half-foot taller.

"Are you sure you're an *advanced* species? This leg doesn't remotely fit me. And you didn't even get the race correct. It belongs on a black man!"

"I will contact the refurb department to request a replacement. Of course, we will have to fill out the appropriate paperwork and return the leg in *like new* condition before they will send another one."

Tara smirked and said, "Too bad they sent a basketball player's leg and not his—"

"Don't go there!" I interrupted. "Will you please do me a favor? Hide all the medical supplies in the bedroom. Take the plastic too. And while you're in there, grab a tall pair of socks from my top dresser drawer and my gray sweatshirt and sweatpants from the closet. Hurry!"

At that moment, I didn't know whether to cry or dance for joy. I truly was Doctor Refurb. And my first superhero feat was to bring my sister back to life!

A car door thumped shut.

Tara threw my clothes at me from the bedroom door.

Amy knocked.

I pulled on my sweatpants and asked, "Rodney, can you please give us some privacy?"

"Under the circumstances, I must stay. But I will be quiet and turn off my visual image while I multitask with the refurb department on a replacement leg. Oh, and Tara, keep in mind that every change to the past creates a new timeline. Some new timelines are virtually identical to their predecessors, and others feature changes that affect almost everyone. Donald Trump's failure to be born most definitely fits into the latter category. Since new timelines can be confusing until your memory catches up, you should know that Amy no longer died before you met her and assume she knows you well." He disappeared.

I took a step toward the front door and fell on my shoulder. I got back up and fell again. This wasn't gonna be easy. The comicalness of it reminded me of King Arthur hopping along on his make-believe horse in *Monty Python and the Holy Grail*. I mimicked his hops—minus coconuts for a sound effect—and made it to the door.

Amy kissed me on the cheek, strutted into the kitchen, leaned down to give Clarice multiple kisses, and glanced back. "What a day! I'm so looking forward to sharing this bottle of wine with you." She gazed across to the living room and swept a lock of auburn hair behind her ear. "Oh! Hi, Tara. Cleaning up after Stefan again? I warned you to run while you had the chance!"

Tara had dropped to her knees to scrub some blood she missed on the throw rug in front of the couch. She casually looked up and said, "What can I say? Stefan has steady hands in the operating room, but at home he's such a klutz."

"I've probably told you this before, but I really like the influence you've had on Stefan. When he first moved into this cabin, he kept it so stark. Now I can see a woman's touch." She pointed to a painting on the wall opposite the couch. "Is that new? I must say, your taste in art is a bit eccentric. The red paint splattered on that woman's face gives it a Maxfield-Parrish-gone-goth feeling." She walked partway into the living room, tilted her head, and laughed. "Oh, never mind! It's just ketchup or something. What did you two do today? Have a food fight?"

"Something like that," Tara said.

Amy looked over her shoulder at me. "Don't just stand there. Get me a wet paper towel. If that ketchup or whatever it is gets any drier, it'll be hell to remove."

"No, no!" Tara said. "You get started on that bottle of wine with your brother. I'll have all this cleaned up in a few minutes."

"That would be rude of us. We'll wait. Clarice is begging to go outside anyway. Come on, Stefan. Let's take her for a short walk." She stepped back into the kitchen and glanced down at my sweatpants. "Since you're already dressed for it, let's make it a run. Do you think you can still beat your little sister in a race? What do ya say—to the road and back? Loser pays for pizza delivery!"

"I can't," I said. "I slipped and twisted my knee earlier today. It hurts to walk."

"Did you ice it?"

"I don't think it needs it."

She pointed to a chair and shook her head. "Sit down and let me have a look at it. Doctors *always* make the worst patients."

"Can you just take Clarice out for me? Please. I promise to have an icepack on my knee by the time you return."

Tara finished scrubbing the rug and tilted toward Amy as she stood. "Grab Clarice's ball on your way out. It's in the basket by the door."

I waited for Amy and Clarice to depart before calling out, "Rodney, where's my replacement?"

A sheepish grin adorned Rodney's face as his image appeared. "I have good news and bad news."

"Why can't you ever have just good news?"

"The bad news is that light-skinned legs in your size are on back order."

"Back order!"

"Sure. Humans are rather arrogant about believing they are 'one of a kind,' but that couldn't be further from the truth. In reality, there are hundreds of thousands of planets across the universe with creatures like you. And those are just the ones my people know about. Recently, there has been a run on refurbished legs for six-foot-tall white men."

"How long are they on back order for?"

"Thirty-five to sixty-five Earth-days."

"I can't live like this for that long!"

"That brings me to the good news. I am just waiting for confirmation from the supply manager on a suitable substitute. Hold on." He disappeared.

I hopped back into the living room and collapsed on the couch.

Tara, who had no choice but to listen in on what Rodney said, set her cleaning materials down and cuddled up to me. "We *will* get through this. . . . Somehow."

Rodney reappeared, dressed as a circus ringmaster. He twirled into a showman pose, with his top hat held high and his cane held low. "I have two matching light-skinned legs on hold for you. The supply manager says they are professional athlete-compatible, with a circumference that is within the acceptable measurements for a proper fit. You will gain a few inches in height, however. But every man wants to be a bit taller, huh?"

"I don't want to lose another leg!"

He tapped his cane on the brim of his hat. "It will be quick. And as part of the upgrade, we will deport Brazilian president Jair Bolsonaro at no extra charge. That is an outstanding value for a current head of state! Naturally, we will deport him early in life, so his disappearance will not become an international incident. Just think of what you will be doing to save the Amazon Rainforest." He took an exaggerated breath. "Some people call the Amazon Rainforest 'the lungs of the planet.' You will be an environmental hero!"

I made eye contact with Tara, and she nodded.

"Can you do it right now?" I asked.

"Just sign the exchange form, and let me know when you are ready," he replied.

I gestured toward the picture window and said to Tara, "Please look outside and see what Amy and Clarice are doing."

She pushed off the couch and peered out the big window before moving to a smaller one on a sidewall. "There they are—

way out in the tall grass, near the Forest Service boundary. They appear to be looking for something."

"Clarice must have lost her ball again. That should give us enough time. Can you grab another plastic bag out of the kitchen for me to sit on? And while you're in there, find something rubber for me to bite down on. I don't think there's enough morphine left in my system to do much good, and I was lucky not to bite through my tongue the last time."

"The only thing I see around here made of rubber is Clarice's chewy bone."

"That'll have to do. Give it a quick rinse first."

"No shit," she said.

I signed the exchange form, and when Tara returned to the living room, I slid the plastic underneath me and slipped the bone between my teeth.

"He's ready," Tara said.

Rodney nodded before looking off into the distance as he called out, "Okay, here we go. On three. One . . . two . . . Oh, lucky you. The supply manager just upgraded you to a complete below the waist set!"

"What!" I screamed, muffled by the bone.

"Three!"

Pain seized my body! I bit down so hard on the rubber bone that it split into three pieces. I passed out for a moment, but this time Tara quickly revived me. There was no time for sleep and, fortunately, the pain was already flowing out of me. That was the one positive I was learning about the process: the pain dissipated once a refurbished part was seated.

As soon as I could concentrate, I scanned around me and confirmed that even though blood had drenched my sweatpants, at least there weren't any splatters on the walls.

While I was doing that, Tara completed a cursory check of my vitals before hurrying into the kitchen to bring back a garbage bag.

I staggered to my feet, tossed into the bag the bloody plastic I was sitting on, then shimmied off my pants and underwear and threw them in too.

Tara tried not to smile as she pointed. "Oh, my! You are quite a bit more . . . athletic. We'll have to try that out after Amy goes home."

I collapsed back onto the couch without any of the amusement Tara was feeling. "Rodney, you asshole! You tricked me. I demand my own penis back!"

"I wish I could help you," he said in a caring voice. "But refurbished body parts can never be exchanged for originals. If you want, I can remove your refurbished member and stimulate regrowth of a new one. If all goes well, you will be as good as new in about a month."

"Fuck that! I quit. Go ahead and wipe our memories. Anything is better than this."

"Are you sure? Your new parts are exceptional specimens that should give you many years of excellent service. You will be able to run faster than you ever could before, and your new penis comes with a lifetime guarantee against erectile dysfunction." He balanced his cane upright on his palm. "Should your penis ever fail, just contact our customer service department for a free replacement!"

"I said, I quit."

Rodney frowned. "All right then. My people are not barbarians. The last thing we want is an unhappy customer. Would you like to say goodbye to your sister before I wipe yours and Tara's memories and revert everything to how it was before we met?"

"How can you do that? You said that once someone reached the depository planet they were irretrievable."

"That is true. Hold on while I contact a supervisor in the

transfer division." He blinked out, only to blink back seconds later. "I have good news! We have been busier than usual lately. In fact, that is one of the reasons I was able to go directly from my training graduation to a full-time planetary consultant, third class. Limbaugh, Trump, and Bolsonaro are all delayed at the transfer facility. Since you seem to be unsure about going forward, I have arranged for them, and anyone else we send there, to be held in stasis until I give the go-ahead for release to the depository planet. Now you will not have any pressure and can quit any time you want. We will even let you keep your refurbished body parts as a *free gift!*"

"But if I quit, Donald Trump will be born and Amy will die?"

"I am afraid so."

I balled my fists and hissed, "Shit, shit, shit!"

Tara looked at me with sympathetic eyes. "You can't quit, Stefan. It's not only your sister who gets to live, but hundreds of thousands of other people too."

I exhaled through gritted teeth before saying, "Fine. But I want an honest answer from you, Rodney. How does this all end?"

"I thought that was clear in the terms and conditions. It ends when all simulations show that your planet is out of danger. I check after each deportation, and you are already making splendid progress."

Clarice barked in the distance.

My eyes widened. "They're coming back! Tara, I'm not comfortable walking on these legs yet. Hide the garbage bag in the bedroom closet and bring me another pair of sweats!"

She raced one way and then the other.

Clarice barked again, a little closer.

I pulled on the clean sweats and Tara filled a bag with ice and tossed it to me. I looked up. "Rodney! Can you give us a break, please?"

He cut off his visual image.

The door opened and Clarice charged in, followed by Amy.

My sister went directly to the cupboard, pulled out three glasses, opened the bottle she brought, and poured the wine. She carried the glasses to the couch and set them on the coffee table. "Oh, good. You've put an ice bag on that knee." Her gaze continued to the floor. "Holy shit! More ketchup? If I didn't know better, I'd swear it was blood. Do you two have a ketchup fetish I should know about?"

Chapter 7

We Can Rebuild Him

Seeing my sister alive, after she had been dead for more than a year, was an experience that exceeded awesome. She was my only sibling, and we had always been close. As her big brother, I was naturally protective of her, and though I was average in size and weight for my age, being two years older than her meant that I was usually bigger than any classmate of hers who gave her trouble. More than once, I had to step in to protect her because she shot her mouth off and told a male classmate to go fuck an amoeba.

Despite the awesomeness of Amy's visit, once we finished the bottle of wine and dinner, I told her I was exhausted and wanted to get to bed early.

My sister took the hint, and Tara and I breathed a sigh of relief as we waved to her while she turned her car around and eased down the driveway.

As we stepped back through the doorway, I said, "I can't believe she thought my blood was ketchup."

"I can't believe she didn't notice you were taller!"

"I slumped a lot."

We moved back to the couch, intending to spend some quiet time together. Clarice waylaid those plans when all sixty pounds of her crash-landed on our laps.

"I think she wants to go outside again," Tara said with a laugh. "I'm sure you're not ready for more than a few steps, so I'll take her."

"No, actually, I'd like to give a longer walk a shot. These legs don't feel like mine, and they will most likely stay that way until I give them some use. Let's take her together, in case I fall and can't get up."

"Okay."

"One thing before we go. Rodney, are you still there?"

He reappeared, wearing an orange hoodie, leaning against an invisible wall, with his ankles crossed. "Yes I am, Stefan. How can I be of assistance?"

"Now that Amy has left, can you disappear for a few days? I need to get used to these legs."

Tara winked at me.

"And I suppose that other extremity as well. We also need time to get up to date with the new state of the world. Neither of us can risk going back to work and being surprised when someone else we thought was dead suddenly appears in person, in a conversation, or on the news."

"That is a reasonable request. I will come back on Wednesday. In the meantime, enjoy your new body parts and think about whom to deport next." He vanished.

For the first time, I stood straight and looked at myself in a mirror. I had gained roughly three inches, and the only footwear I owned that accommodated my larger feet was a pair of sport sandals with adjustable straps. I was going to have to shop for pants and shoes before showing up at work or anywhere else people knew me. I was also going to have to come up with a plausible explanation for my sudden growth spurt.

We donned jackets and headlamps, and with Tara holding onto my arm, we stepped outside. The fall sky was already dark, and the cool air was vigorously warning that winter was on its way.

We proceeded slowly down my long driveway, wary of Clarice dancing around us. At twenty yards, Tara asked, "How do you feel?"

"Better than I expected. Believe it or not, the trickiest part is getting used to having larger feet, not longer legs."

The farther we walked, the steadier I became. When we turned onto the gravel road at the end of the driveway, I asked Tara to release my arm. As we continued our walk, I paused several times to try various movements. Squatting for the first time in years without feeling pain in my knees made me reconsider my aversion to refurbished limbs.

"Let's pick up the pace," I said.

"Are you sure you won't fall on your face? I've already cleaned up enough of your blood for one day."

"My balance isn't quite what I'd like it to be. After all, I'm way up here. Even so, my legs feel strong—even stronger than my original legs. I'd kind of like to see what they can do."

We started with a slow jog.

I fell on my face.

I picked myself up—no blood—and continued on.

"Faster," I said.

Clarice cut in front of me, and I fell again.

I returned to my feet and repeated, "Faster."

"I won't be able to keep up," Tara panted.

"Wait here if you want. I'm gonna run to the highway and back."

"That's almost a mile!" she said, as she slowed to a walk.

I clipped along at what felt like three-quarters speed. Since Clarice was keeping up with me, I pushed it a little more, until she was running as fast as she could.

I was flying! Not literally, of course.

I tripped and launched forward with what felt like impressive hang-time—until my chin scraped gravel. Clarice jumped on me, thinking it was a big game, and added another scratch to my face.

I got back up and continued to the highway before turning around and running toward Tara. As I ran, I thought about the *Six Million Dollar Man* TV series reruns I used to watch as a child. The opening words for each episode repeated in my head: "Gentlemen, we can rebuild him. We have the technology. . . ." I couldn't mimic the bionic sound effect precisely. Instead, I chanted, "Nah-nah-na-na-na-na," and added just enough speed that Clarice dropped a few lengths behind me.

As I reached Tara, I shouted, "Holy shit!"

"Holy shit is right," she said. "I've never seen anyone run so fast!"

"How fast do you think I was going?"

"I couldn't accurately guess, because you were coming toward me."

"I've never clocked Clarice, but I bet she can do better than thirty, and she was struggling to keep up. When Rodney said my new parts were exceptional specimens, I didn't think he meant they were enhanced, like the toenail. And with more practice and proper footwear, I know I can run even faster."

She looked at me and purred, "Shall we test your other appendage to see if it's enhanced too?"

I scowled. "I know you think you're being cute and funny and all, but there's literally no man on Earth who would be turned on by 'Oh, your new penis is so much better than your previous one!' Besides, I think we should find out just how enhanced it is before putting it into action."

"I'm sorry."

"No worries. It's been a long and traumatic day, and I'm probably a bit more sensitive than I should be. Right now, I'm gonna walk over to that tree and see how this new appendage does at marking my territory. Then I wanna go to bed with you—and cuddle. Tomorrow night, we'll make sure my new penis is firmly attached before slowly and carefully trying it out together. I promise."

She burst into laughter. "I hadn't thought about it that way. Your penis falling off at the wrong time would be a real mood-breaker, wouldn't it? Still, the mental picture of it. . . ." She tilted her head and stared off into space. "Oh, never mind!"

Chapter 8

All the Dead People

T he following day, we slept in and then went shopping. Although sometimes it felt as if Tara and I had been together for our entire lives, we had only been a couple for five months. As such, we hadn't gone clothes shopping together before. While it might be too broad of a generalization to say every woman wants to redo her man, personal experience and chats with male friends tell me it happens frequently.

One survival technique I learned from nine years of marriage is that shopping goes much smoother if you just accept that resistance is futile. Consequently, I mostly hung out in the dressing room while Tara brought me shoes and pants to try on.

Only when she started bringing me shirts did I put a refurbished foot down. "We don't know where this is going. My upper body could look like Pee-wee Herman's or the Incredible Hulk's by the time this is over."

"I don't think you'll ever look like the Hulk," she said with a wry smile.

I exhaled a frustrated breath. "I wasn't being literal. But if not the Hulk, how about Arnold Schwarzenegger?"

"Oh, do you expect to age thirty-five years too?"

"I'm pretty sure this shopping trip has already aged me halfway there."

"Just try on this one shirt. Come on. You'll look sexy in it."

"Fine."

We returned to the cabin with several bags of clothes. None of them containing anything I would have selected had I gone shopping by myself.

As much as I complained, when I thought about the efforts Tara took every day to look good for me, returning the favor by wearing some clothes she liked seemed like a fair exchange.

And the fact that she hadn't freaked out by the events of the past few days made me realize just how important she was to me. I couldn't ask for a better teammate in what we were going through. I loved her so much it hurt.

* * *

Now that I had shoes and pants that fit, next on our list was to drive back to the cabin, pour coffees, and sit at the kitchen table while we searched the internet to catch up on what life was like without the damage caused by Donald Trump and Jair Bolsonaro.

Neither Tara nor I knew anyone in Brazil, so there was no danger of us being surprised by someone from there we thought was dead who was now alive. Also, since all records of what-once-was instantly changed when Bolsonaro was deported, we only had our memories to go on. Neither of us could remember how many Brazilians had died of COVID-19 before the change, but we both remembered that the country was second in total deaths worldwide—just behind the United States. We also couldn't remember how much of the Amazon rainforest had been destroyed under Bolsonaro. That said, learning that Brazil now ranked fourteenth in total COVID-19 deaths, and that the country's current president was much more conservation-oriented than Bolsonaro had been, assured us that the change had created an improvement well worth the leg it cost me.

As we continued our research, I wondered why Tara and I kept our memories of the previous timeline. For instance, if Donald Trump never existed, how could we remember him? My best guess was that Rodney had something to do with it. If he had the power to instantly amputate a leg and replace it with a refurbished one, he certainly had the power to put some sort of bubble around us that protected our physical location and memories from timeline changes. After all, each person on Earth affected someone who affected another, who affected another, who affected another, and so on. If we didn't have some level of timeline-change resistance, anyone we deported—whether famous or not—had the potential to make it so Tara and I wouldn't know each other or remember why a guy named Rodney was occupying our brains.

Recognizing even a fraction of the improvements to life on Earth because Donald Trump never existed was more challenging than we expected. Even in the original timeline, Trump's presidency had consisted of a daily barrage of lies, bigotry, self-centeredness, hate, and incompetence that was impossible to keep up with. He would do something unethical on Monday and follow it up with something despicable on Tuesday that would make most people forget all about Monday's transgression. It was his gift, in an evil sort of way.

Therefore, as I researched on my laptop and Tara researched on her smartphone, we tossed back and forth what we found and eventually came to several rather broad conclusions. Immediately evident to both of us was that the United States was a friendlier place. While Democrats and Republicans still disagreed on practically everything, violence was way down. This we attributed to the fact that Trump wasn't around to give fascists, white supremacists, and other hate groups permission to come out from under their rocks.

Additionally, the sometimes violent anti-mask, anti-vaccine movement never took hold as it had in the timeline occupied by Donald Trump. This we attributed to President Hillary Clinton's quick action on COVID-19. Consequently, the United States now ranked twenty-second in COVID-19 deaths, compared to the first in deaths ranking it had in the Trump timeline. Unfortunately, Rodney's simulation, predicting Clinton as a one-term president, held true. Without Americans being able to witness how bad the pandemic had been under Trump, Republican Ted Cruz won the 2020 presidential election by convincing just enough voters that the relatively low death numbers were because of America's superior medical facilities, not "Clinton's economy-damaging shutdown and strict mask requirements." Nevertheless, once he took office, President Ted Cruz renamed many of Clinton's virus-fighting programs and adapted them as his own.

Both of us also searched the names of everyone we personally knew who died of COVID-19. Some were, indeed, *still dead*. Others, including Ron Mitchell, a good friend of mine from med school, were now alive. I looked forward to calling him when this was all over.

Since Rodney had declared that body parts for deportations wouldn't end until Earth was out of danger, I doubted he was too concerned about Donald Trump's fascist deeds or the lives his arrogance had destroyed. And since Republicans undid most of Hillary Clinton's environmental progress once she was out of office, I wondered why deporting Fred Trump was approved so quickly. All replacing President Donald Trump with President Hillary Clinton did for the environment was cause a four-year delay in Republican ass-kissing legislation for fossil fuels corporations.

Tara and I were discussing just that when she exclaimed, "It's all the dead people!"

"Why would you say that?" I asked. "Let's say two hundred thousand more Americans are alive today because Clinton jumped on the pandemic early and didn't create mask or vaccine controversies. Many of those people are going to have children, and those children are going to have children, etcetera. Within a few generations, the population increase will be in the millions. More people will mean more pressure on natural resources and the environment. From a purely cold, scientific viewpoint, I would argue that Trump actually helped the planet."

"Yes, but only if all those people were unexceptional. You can't get caught up in the fact that most of the COVID-19 patients you've watched die at your hospital had refused to get vaccinated and believed in a wide variety of kooky conspiracy theories. Really, all it would take was the death of one unlucky but brilliant scientist or inventor to turn the whole equation around. Imagine if COVID-19 took the life of someone before she invented a toaster-sized battery that could power a car for a thousand miles without recharging, or took the life of someone before she figured out how to make an inexpensive cake-pan-sized solar panel that could power a large house."

I shook my head. "Ooh, I didn't see it that way. This is why we make such a good team."

"Are we done analyzing how life on Earth has improved without Bolsonaro and Trump?" she asked.

"I think so. But we should still spend some more time reading on-line newspapers and magazines to catch up on what is now a very different world for us."

She raised an eyebrow. "We should also keep an eye out for that brilliant scientist or inventor."

"That too."

"Have you thought about who we should deport next?"

"Coming up with that person has never left my mind, and I think I have the environmental villain to bring this entire, gruesome endeavor to a close."

"Who?"

I took a sip of coffee before answering over the brim, "Ronald Reagan."

"Ronald Reagan?"

"Yes. I wrote an essay on him in college. Few presidents have had their legacy whitewashed as thoroughly as his was. Until Trump came along, he was the president Republicans revered as a demigod."

Tara tilted her head back to swallow the last drop of liquid in her cup before asking, "But was Reagan really worse on the environment than any of the other Republican presidents of the past fifty or so years?"

"Oh, without a doubt. Before him, Republican presidents weren't nearly as militant at opposing environmental progress. Richard Nixon, for example, signed into law some of the most important environmental legislation in American history. Then came Reagan, who called the solar panels Jimmy Carter had installed on the White House roof 'a joke' and had them removed. That single act inspired a Republican lovefest with corporate polluters that continues to this day."

"I didn't know about the solar panels," she said.

"Few people today do. But sometimes big changes arise from seemingly minor events. For Republicans, removing the solar panels became a powerful symbolic statement that encouraged them to cheer on the oil, gas, and coal industries. And Reagan hammered home his point by gutting the research and development budgets for renewable energy at the Department of Energy and eliminating tax breaks for solar and wind power, thereby crippling renewable energy development for more than a decade."

Tara got up from the table and set her empty cup in the sink.

"Wow! I knew Republicans had favored fossil fuels over renewable energy during my entire lifetime. Now I finally understand why."

"Yes, and after Reagan paved the way, lack of ethics, excessive greed, and support from fossil fuels-funded super PACs all combined to keep Republicans speeding along that same dirty road."

"Let's get Reagan!"

Chapter 9

Bedtime for Ronny

Rodney returned on Wednesday, as we were putting lunch on the table. "Knock! Knock! Good afternoon humans," he said with a too-bright smile.

Even for someone with Rodney's advanced powers, apparently there was no gradual way to enter our brains. Tara and I both jumped when it happened.

"Good afternoon, Rodney," we replied in unison, with sarcasm he apparently didn't notice.

"Are you ready for our next deportation?"

"Yes," I said. "Ronald Reagan."

"Ooh, that is a savvy choice. Trying to wrap this all up in one ultimate move, I see."

"Have you been listening in on our conversations?" I asked.

He pushed out his belly and cradled it with both hands. "Just think of me as Santa Claus. I see you when you're sleeping, I know when you're awake, and I know if you've been bad or good. And I must say that during the past two nights both of you were *very* bad! Stefan, you had me a little worried for a while, but once you overcame the fear that your new penis would fall off or explode, it performed beyond your expectations. Am I right? And Tara," he playfully shook a finger, "if I had actual ears, they would be ringing right now."

"You're a third class pig," I said.

"Perhaps. But someday I will be a first class pig."

"No doubt," Tara said.

"Hey, I know neither of you likes me. No one likes their planetary consultant . . . at least at first. But when I say I am concerned about your satisfaction, I say that with all sincerity." Rodney's hoodie morphed into a white lab coat, and a clipboard loaded with paper materialized in his left hand. With his right hand, he pulled a pen from behind his ear and tapped its tip on the paper. "Therefore, I would like to know if you have had any physical problems with your new extremities."

"None at all," Tara said quickly.

I cleared my throat. "I think he was asking me. So Rodney, I'll answer your question with a question. Why are all of my new parts performing beyond human specifications?"

He jotted a note before replying, "Remember earlier, when I said that it was rather arrogant of Earth-humans to think they were 'one of a kind,' and that there are actually hundreds of thousands of planets across the universe with creatures like you?"

"Yes."

"Well, even though you all started out biologically similar, environmental factors such as gravity, air quality, and diet, all played a part in human development. Consequently, humans on different planets have evolved different characteristics. Some may be stronger; some may be weaker; some may be healthier; some may be sicker; some may be smarter; and the list goes on. When my people began serving as planetary consultants for thousands of human populations, the variables frustrated the technicians in our refurbishing department so much that they filed a complaint with their supervisors. That led to an agreement, which allowed them to set all biological components to match the most superior human components we had encountered. After all, who is going to fill out a customer service survey and complain that they are better than they were before? In short, your new parts are performing within human specifications—just not Earth-human specifications."

I wasn't sure how to respond to this new information, so I simply said, "Shall we get on with it?"

"Very well. On what date would you like to deport Ronald Reagan?"

"I'm not sure. I guess any time before his political career begins."

Tara's eyes lit up. "I know! Right after he starred in *Bedtime for Bonzo*."

"*Bedtime for Bonzo?*" I asked. "Making that his last movie will mean that's all people will remember him for."

She chuckled. "It's my gift to the world."

Rodney flashed a palm and said, "Hold on, while I run simulations to predict if Ronald Reagan's deportation will lead us closer to our goal and not eliminate either of you."

"We need at least a half hour to get ready anyway, so take your time," I said.

He vanished.

We finished our lunch before moving to the living room, where I ripped open a fresh plastic garbage bag to catch my blood and settled in on the couch. Tara administered a shot of morphine.

When Rodney reappeared, we burst into laughter. Instead of his usual Trevor Noah look, he had taken on the form of a chimpanzee dressed in human clothing. He bounced from side to side inside our heads before announcing, "I am back! Everything checks out. Simulations show outstanding progress toward saving your world, and neither of you has any biological connection to the former president. Just nod and we will get started."

The brief humorous moment Rodney provided us gave way to one of seriousness. I smiled nervously at Tara as I waited for the morphine to kick in.

I nodded.

Blood spurted across the room!

I screamed in pain! "Oh, fuck! You took my eye! Fu—"

I passed out.

Chapter 10

The Preacher President

When I awoke, an hour or so later, Tara had already bandaged my eye socket and was busy cleaning up blood spatters. I could see her clearly with my left eye and Rodney—back in his usual form—in a void where my right eye used to be.

Rodney realized I was awake first and said, "I have good news and bad news."

"Fuck you," I managed to whisper. "Here we go again."

"The good news is that an eye grows back quicker than a leg. You can expect your sight restored in about four weeks, though I cannot guarantee twenty-twenty vision."

"Wha . . . what if I have to operate on someone in the meantime?" I paused to let my mind clear. "I can survive day-to-day life with one eye, but I don't think I'd have the precision to perform delicate surgery."

"Before I answer that, let me get to the bad news, which, depending on how you look at it, can be good news too."

I swallowed hard and waited for him to continue.

"While you were unconscious, I had the chance to check out the results of our Ronald Reagan deportation. The vast majority of my pre-deportation simulations were extremely promising. With Reagan gone, it was highly likely that Jimmy Carter would be reelected president and able to continue with four more years of strong environmental policies. A few simulations showed George H. W. Bush defeating Carter, but even his policies were not as damaging to the environment as Reagan's were. But alas, as advanced as my simulation programs are, they are not infallible." He nervously chuckled. "You will never guess who won the 1980 Presidential Election."

I readjusted myself on the couch and asked, "Who?"

"Pat Robertson!"

"No way!"

"Yes way," Rodney replied. "Since the Republicans did not have a celebrity father-figure candidate to oppose Carter, Robertson filled the void by cashing in on his similar qualities and running for president earlier than he did in the previous timeline. Politically, it turned out to be a brilliant move, because in the Republican primary most of the people who would have voted for Reagan ended up voting for Robertson. Then, a week before the general election, eleven major evangelists simultaneously announced that Jesus had come to them in a dream with a warning that the USSR would launch an all-out surprise nuclear attack on the United States unless Robertson was elected president. Just enough people believed the well-coordinated scam for Robertson to eke out a victory."

"So what's the bottom line?" I asked.

"The bottom line is that in many ways, President Pat Robertson was even worse on the environment than Ronald Reagan was. While raking in money from the oil and coal industries, he would simply repeat his slogan, 'God will fix it,' whenever situations arose that were beyond his grasp. That allowed Robertson to ignore problems—especially environmental ones— while creating an ideology that demanded his Christian followers ignore his incompetence. After all, blaming Robertson for a failure would be the equivalent of blaming God for that same failure."

"You mean I lost an eye for nothing?"

"I am afraid so. But like I said, it is kind of good news too."

"How so?"

"Since my simulation program made the mistake, my supervisor has approved a refurbished replacement for you from our Rapid Return Body Part Service."

"Let me guess. The new eye will give me telescopic vision."

"No. That would be stupid. Humans everywhere are perfectly capable of using binoculars whenever they need them. Night vision, however, is much more useful, and that is something humans living on a slowly rotating planet have evolved. In the dark, your new eyes will allow you to see almost as clearly as an owl can."

"Eyes?"

"We can't very well leave Pat Robertson as president, can we?"

"Fuck me," I said under my breath.

Tara was blotting up some blood that had reached the armrest opposite me. I put a hand on her shoulder to get her attention and said, "It's too late now, because I will overdose, but the next time we do this, let's skip the morphine and go directly to the fentanyl."

She paused long enough to nod before going back to work.

I continued. "Rodney, before we do this, please verify that your Rapid Return Body Part Service has in stock two matching eyes in my size and color. I can't suddenly have eyes from some humongous human that bug out on my face, like a tarsier's."

"I will do that at the same time I run new simulations and make sure that neither of you is Pat Robertson's secret love child. Hold on."

As soon as he disappeared, Tara dropped the rag she was cleaning with into a bucket and asked, "Do you trust him?"

"Hell no. But you know what I trust even less?"

"What?"

"That either he or his people actually have the power to make whatever they take from me grow back. This is the third time something has come up to make giving me a refurbished replacement the most desirable option."

"Do you think Rodney is listening in on us now?"

"Perhaps. After he confessed to at least listening to us having sex, I've pretty much given up on having any privacy until this is all over."

"We haven't confirmed whether he can see what we see, however. That might come in handy if we ever need to keep a secret. We can just write it down."

Rodney reappeared. "Everything has been taken care of. We have a nice pair of refurbished night-vision-capable blue eyes in your size, and they are ready for transplant. On the political side, I recommend deporting Pat Robertson in 1964, right after all his children were born. That will give us the best chance of keeping any unexpected timeline changes to a minimum. My simulations still favor Jimmy Carter defeating George H. W. Bush in the presidential election. If they hold, we should be back on track for a major improvement in Earth's long-term health."

"Okay, let's get this over with," I said.

Chapter 11

Foodies

F ollowing the customary blood spurts, screams of pain, oh fucks, and loss of consciousness, I awoke with a new set of eyes.

From my position on the couch, I looked at objects around the room to test my sight. Everything was in perfect focus. But what about the night vision Rodney had promised? Since the sun had already set, I shuffled over to the picture window and gazed across my yard and into the forest. "Tara, come here." She walked in from the kitchen and stood next to me. I pointed. "Can you see that coyote standing at the edge of the tall grass between those two trees?"

"No. All I see is a wall of black."

"That's what I thought. These new eyes are amazing. Not only can they see in the dark, but they also keep everything in sharp focus—both near and far."

Rodney returned from wherever he had gone. "I am so glad you are happy with your new eyes! While you were asleep, I checked the current timeline and updated Earth's habitability expiration date. This time Jimmy Carter really did get reelected, and overall you have added at least sixty years of viable life to your planet. Congratulations!"

"Thanks.... I think."

"I hear the hesitancy in your voice. You are disappointed that your mission is not complete. I feel the same way. I will not get a promotion to full-time planetary consultant, first class, until this is over either. With that in mind, I took the liberty of running numerous simulations to come up with a variety of effective recommendations for you. For instance, a logical move would be to deport some political leaders from China. After all, no other country pollutes more than they do. Unfortunately, I went all the way back to the founding of the People's Republic of China, and every leader I simulated deporting was seamlessly replaced by another who supported the identical policies. The same goes for Saudi Arabia. One by one, we could deport all the members of the royal family, from the King on down, and never come up with someone who would lead the country in an environmentally sustainable direction."

"I'm not surprised," I said. "That's the advantage of an authoritarian government—stability."

"I'm actually relieved," Tara added. "Stefan doesn't have enough body parts to even consider China or Saudi Arabia."

Tara and I moved from the window to the couch as Rodney continued. "What my simulations suggest is that we concentrate on nonpoliticians, such as Karl Benz, who invented the first car with an internal combustion engine, and Henry Ford, whose mass-produced Model T dealt a death blow to a burgeoning electric automobile industry. We will never stop all fossil fuels technologies, but we can slow them down enough to give cleaner alternatives the upper hand."

"I'd have a hard time justifying deporting someone who was just an inventor," I said. "If I'm going to give up a body part, that person must be obviously greedy, evil, or corrupt. What about oil company executives? Surely there are many who meet all three requirements."

"We can consider them too, but as Tara accurately stated, you only have a limited number of body parts."

"Then let's give up this entire body parts exchange charade! It's sick; it's painful; and since you're now making suggestions and simulating every move before we make it, your earlier excuse of forcing me to give up body parts to keep me from going hog-wild and deporting undeserving people just doesn't hold water. What's really going on here?"

"Hold on." He vanished.

Tara walked into the kitchen, grabbed a notepad from the counter, wrote something, and returned to the couch to show it to me: *I think you have him rattled. Perhaps we'll get to the bottom of this once and for all.*

I took the pad to jot a response, but Rodney returned before I could write a word.

He frowned and said, "My supervisor is quite upset. She almost wiped your memories back to childhood and canceled this entire project. I am afraid if you do not start trusting me that is exactly what she will do." A halo pinged above his head.

"Trust is earned, not forced upon someone by threat," I said.

"I got you your sister back, didn't I?" He smiled and pointed up. His halo pinged again.

I ignored Rodney's special effect and said, "Yes, and you get major points for that. Still, the best way to gain Tara's and my trust is to be straight with us. For instance, you can't really stimulate my body to regrow whatever parts you take from me, can you?"

"Actually, I can. But the new parts are often inferior to the originals. That is especially the case with extremities like legs. They do not grow back as robust, and you would have to complete months of exercise and physical therapy before you

69

could use them normally. And since our customer service department would have to provide you with a specialist trained in virtual physical therapy, a grow-back program would be quite expensive. Therefore, while ethics require me to offer you a regrow option, I am trained to push you into accepting refurbished units."

"Okay, I buy that. But why are you even taking my body parts? What's ethical about that?"

He waved his halo away and said, "You do not want to know."

"Yes, I do."

"Can't you just accept the fact that I really, truly am helping you to save your planet?"

"Nope."

"Open a blank document in your laptop and relax your arms." His visual image disappeared.

I retrieved my computer from the kitchen table and returned to the couch. As my fingers started typing, Tara leaned over to read along: *I am more than just an image in your head. I can see, hear, and feel everything you do. You will be relieved to know that I can turn off any sense whenever I want to. For instance, I turn off sight and sound when you go to the bathroom. Hey, I understand your need for occasional privacy, and I apologize for being a bit of a voyeur the first two times you had sex with your new penis. In those instances, I needed to make sure the refurbished unit was functioning properly and took advantage of the situation to satisfy my curiosity about what copulating felt like for a human—first from a male perspective; then from a female perspective. I will not do that again. Output from whatever senses I am using goes directly to my supervisor and—as Tara guessed earlier—is recorded for quality and training purposes. However, since my supervisor is responsible for multiple planetary consultants and has a life outside of work, she only monitors the feed when she can and gets the rest of the information via my reports. Touch-typing is the one way I can communicate with you and have little chance of being monitored. Now that you know that, I am going to reveal to you why we require your body parts, but you cannot react verbally, either now or in the future. If you agree, clear your throat.*

I cleared my throat.

He typed: *We eat them.*

Tara's eyes grew wide. She retched and covered her mouth! My medical experience kept me from doing the same thing. Instead, my face burned with anger.

Since I knew Rodney had his sense of sight turned off, or at least wasn't looking through my eyes, I couldn't type and answer back. With no silent way of communicating with him, I simply whispered, "Why?"

Rodney typed: *I am going to anticipate a few of your questions; then we are going to change the subject. First, I am not the one eating you. The only people who eat human flesh are the most elite in our society. To use an Earth term, they are "foodies." And just like the elite in any society, they crave what others cannot afford. You may be wondering: why don't they just eat a hunk of refurbished thigh? To our elite, that would be like a foodie on your planet drinking instant coffee. Also, the humans from whom we acquire the parts for refurbishing have already died of natural causes. Fresh flesh is more succulent. This may all seem unethical to you, but to them, they are just eating a lower species —the equivalent to humans on your planet eating whale meat. Despite what you may think, our people have a strong code of ethics. As they see it, in exchange for your providing them with a rare delicacy, they are making you better than you were before and saving your planet at the same time. It is a win-win!*

After Rodney finished typing, Tara and I sat silently for a moment. Then I wiggled my hands, so she knew I had regained control of them, and typed: *Rodney, if you are reading this, turn off visual until I clear my throat. Tara, I feel like I've made a deal with the devil. But that deal has gotten me my sister back, saved countless lives, and appears to be on the way to saving our planet. Considering all that we are getting in return, does it really matter what happens to my original legs, eyes, or anything else Rodney's people amputate from me? At least now, we've solved some of the mystery of why this is all happening. We need to continue.*

She took my laptop and typed: *I'll try not to miss the toilet if I throw up while thinking about this. Other than that, I'm with you. I still believe Rodney is holding something back. XXXOOO*

Chapter 12

The Proposal

I nodded to Tara and cleared my throat.

Rodney's visual image returned. "Are you ready to move on?"

I yawned from the couch and said, "It's late. People on your planet may not need to sleep, but those on mine do."

"Time is different for me than it is for you. In the time it took you to exchange notes with Tara on your laptop, I did some deep thinking, came up with a fresh approach, ran some simulations, and gained the enthusiastic support of my supervisor." He did a giddy little dance. "I have a new proposal for both of you!"

"*Both* of us?" I asked. "Okay, we're listening."

"Since you seem unwilling to deport Henry Ford and other early automotive pioneers, I suggest three things. First, we concentrate on the United States. We already know that deportations are unlikely to slow down pollution from authoritarian countries like China or Saudi Arabia, but simulations do suggest those countries will follow the United States' lead—especially if it is profitable for them. Second, if we are to concentrate on the United States, we must stop climate change denial early, before it becomes an ingrained Republican belief. And finally, if we get close enough to our goal, I have a time travel mission for you that I guarantee will wrap everything up, if successful."

"Time travel?" I asked. "How is that possible?"

"I am surprised you would ask that, after we have already gone back in time to deport Rush Limbaugh, Fred Trump, Jair Bolsonaro, Ronald Reagan, and Pat Robertson."

"Yeah, but none of those maneuvers required a living person from the present to travel physically to another time and then return," I said.

"The science of time travel is too complicated for you to understand. Rather than get bogged down on that, just go along with me this time when I say, 'My people work in mysterious ways.'"

Tara spoke up, "Since you mentioned both of us, does that mean you want me to time travel with Stefan?"

"That is up to you. Only on the rarest occasions do my people directly interact with more than one representative on a planet-saving mission. Time travel is safer in pairs, however, and fixing Earth has become much more complicated than expected. Those complications could be partly because of my inexperience as a planetary consultant, but more than likely, Earth just has an excessive number of unethical people who are willing to do anything for money and power."

"I'm in," Tara said.

He raised a finger. "Not so fast. Both you and Stefan will need skin specially refurbished for the journey."

"Why?" she asked.

"I cannot tell you until we are close enough to our goal for the time travel mission to make a difference."

She nodded. "Will changing my skin be the only requirement?"

"That is also up to you. Being faster and stronger than

everyone else can be a real asset when you are outnumbered and at least temporarily trapped in a time that is not your own."

"She's *not* in," I said.

Tara glared at me. "That's *not* for you to decide."

Rodney flashed an amused smile. "Before either of you commits to anything, I am ethically bound to give you one more slice of information."

"What's that?" I asked.

"Getting into your refurbished skin is going to be much more painful than a quick eye or leg transplant. Instead of feeling the pain in a localized area, you will feel it over your entire body, and skin-tone matching will slow down the process."

I pushed off the couch and walked over to the picture window. As I stared through the darkness, I spotted the coyote again, now joined by four playful pups. My heart ached at the thought of all the animals who had already paid the price for human greed and ignorance. If Earth continued on its path toward mass extinction, life would only get worse for them. "Okay. Say we do all that you propose, but our time travel mission is unsuccessful. What happens then?"

"Before we start, my supervisor will provide me with a budget deemed sufficient to keep sending you back until you are either successful or die. Should you die, you won't care what happens. Should you deplete the budget, caring what happens won't matter either, because my supervisor will almost certainly dismiss Earth as a lost cause and recommend it for recycling."

"When and where will we be time traveling to?" I asked.

"That too will have to wait until we are close enough to our goal for any time travel mission to make a difference. And, perhaps, if we are lucky, we will be so effective with our upcoming deportations that such a mission won't even be neces-sary. Trust me. Because of the pain and danger involved, time travel should only be an option if we are absolutely sure it will push your planet over the finish line."

I rejoined Tara on the couch and asked, "What's our next move?"

Rodney assumed a thoughtful expression and said, "We know that Ronald Reagan gave generations of Republicans permission to favor fossil fuels over renewable energy. Therefore, in the time-line resulting from him being gone, think tanks have had to work harder than ever to convince the American public that human-caused climate change is a hoax. We will have to disband the think tanks that are most influential. If we cannot do that, then we will have to approach from the opposite side and somehow convince newspapers and television networks to stop their lazy practice of quoting think tanks as a way to provide balance to their stories."

"Haven't think tanks been around for a long time?" Tara asked.

I glanced down and realized that Tara's and my hands had unconsciously found each other. I gave hers a slight squeeze and said, "Sure, and not all of them are bad. Some provide valuable research. But many are just well-funded lobbying groups that disseminate lies as factual news stories. For instance, think tanks have advocated for everything from smoking to war, and many are also convenient conduits for foreign countries wishing to buy influence."

"With that in mind, Stefan," Rodney said, "I propose deporting the Koch brothers without delay. That should eliminate both the Cato Institute and Americans for Prosperity. It is an efficient two-at-once deal that will improve your world in multiple ways and be a nice one-two punch for you."

The slight rise in Rodney's eyebrows when he said "one-two punch" prepared me for what was about to happen. I gave Tara's hands another squeeze and said, "The fentanyl, please."

She started for the bathroom before pausing to look over her shoulder and ask, "Lozenge or injection?"

"Injection. Fifty micrograms."

The rest was becoming routine: plastic bags, a change of clothes, and cleaning supplies. In retrospect, I suppose if we had really thought things through, we would have moved to the bathtub or, even better, purchased one of those plastic sauna suits some people wear to lose weight while they work out. One thing was for sure: a new couch and throw rug were in my future.

Rodney allowed some time for the fentanyl to take effect before saying, "I have already arranged for a teenage deportation of the Koch brothers, while they are on a fishing trip. Also, I am obligated to remind you that a grow-back option is available upon your request. For the fastest and least painful recovery, however, I strongly recommend that you take advantage of our refurbished service."

"Refurb will be fine, Rodney."

"Nod when you are ready."

I nodded and didn't even wait for the pain to hit before I started screaming.

Chapter 13

Speak Softly

I awoke with a new set of arms, and I must say that since I pretty much knew what to expect, they were kind of cool. They weren't Arnold Schwarzenegger size—that would have looked stupid on me—but I was reasonably sure they were stronger than Arnold's arms were when he was a body builder. And hey, one could argue that a workout program that involved less than a minute of extreme pain and passing out on a couch was better than one that involved many years of mild pain and passing checks over a counter at a gym.

Tara had just sopped up the last bit of my blood and thrown the dirty rag in a bucket when I asked, "Has Rodney checked the results yet?"

"He disappeared right after your new arms appeared. I assume that's what he's doing now. In the meantime, I'm getting damn tired of cleaning up after you. I was serious when I said I was in. It's time for *you* to clean up after *me* for a change."

A slight twitch at the corner of Tara's lips told me she wasn't as upset about our unequal division of labor as her words indicated. Even so, she had always demanded equality in our relationship—a demand I fully supported, despite my having to rein in my desire to protect her from time to time.

"I agree. You have just as much right to get your arms and legs ripped off as I do. Go ahead and ask Rodney if he'll allow us to switch places for a while. I will be happy to clean up after you."

I stood and began looking for something I could lift or crush to test my new strength. Rodney delayed that test when he materialized inside my head. I sat back down.

He reached forward, as if to shake an invisible hand. "Congratulations! You have added six more years of viable life to your planet. Isn't it amazing how destructive two wealthy brothers and their think tanks can be?"

"I'm glad we're making progress," I said.

"Good! Shall we take down another think tank? Perhaps the Heartland Institute? David Padden and Joseph Bast would give you another two-at-once opportunity. However, I am obligated to inform you that this time you will be sacrificing your ears, and they will be the last external parts we take. After that, we will be moving on to internal organs."

"So are you just taking my outer ears?" I asked.

Rodney frowned. "You know, I did not check. Now that I think about it, my supervisor probably intends to take the middle and inner parts too." He shrugged. "I guess you will find out when it happens."

Tara announced, "Rodney, we need to change things up a bit. Stefan still has enough fentanyl in him that a small additional dose will get him through eliminating the Heartland Institute, but we can't keep pumping him full of painkillers. Both of us also need some sleep. You've already agreed to let me be a part of this, so after the ear exchange, let's take a break. Then, when we pick up later, it's my turn. I'm reaching the age where I'm developing cellulite on my thighs anyway. Let's get rid of it."

"Your thighs do not have any cellulite!" I said in playful protest. "Believe me. I've examined every inch of them."

"Oh, that's sweet of you to say, but they have gobs of it."

I shook my head. "They don't, Rodney. Really."

"Shall we proceed?" Rodney asked.

Tara put two fingers on my wrist and said, "One moment. I wanna check Stefan's pulse before I give him another injection."

"While you're at it, just put a garbage bag over my head. It'll make cleaning up a hell of a lot easier."

"I will not! Besides, Clarice would be disappointed."

"Disappointed? Why?"

She grinned. "You'll find out when it's my turn."

Tara gave me an injection, and Rodney whooshed my outer, middle, and inner ears off to some foodies in a galaxy far, far away.

Not being able to hear myself scream until the refurbish replacements were seated was both weird and unsatisfying.

* * *

When I awoke, sounds dominated my world—a dripping faucet, the refrigerator running, Tara's heartbeat, a dog lapping. "Clarice! No!" I hissed.

"It's okay," Tara assured. "It's only water."

"Ow! Not so loud."

"Actually, I was speaking softly. Now I'm barely whispering. Before Rodney disappeared, he warned me that you'd be sensitive to sounds. I am to reassure you that even though your hearing has improved to roughly the equivalent of Clarice's, just as normal sounds aren't painful for her, they won't be painful for you either. That is, once your brain adjusts to your new ears."

"How long will that adjustment take?"

"I'm not sure. Certainly less time than it will take me to adjust to your new Barack Obama look."

"What?" I tried to make a break for the bathroom, but Tara pushed me back down.

"I'm kidding. Your ears look exactly as they did before."

Rodney popped in. "Congratulations! You have added four more years of viable life to your planet. We are making steady progress. Now I will give you that break you asked for and return on Friday morning." His image blinked out and back in. "Oh, Tara. Before I depart, do you have someone in mind for your first sacrifice, or should I come up with a recommendation for you?"

She looked up. "I know exactly who I want, and if deporting him doesn't add at least twenty-five years to life on Earth, your projections are worthless."

"Who?"

"Rupert Murdoch."

He nodded approvingly and vanished.

Chapter 14

Girls Don't Pass Out

Friday began Tara's weekend of terror. She was correct about deporting a young Rupert Murdoch. That deportation eliminated the Fox News Channel and added twenty-nine years of viable life to Planet Earth. Following him, we moved on to the fossil fuels industry and deported the worst of the worst.

By noon on Sunday, Tara was identical to me in refurbished body parts—except for the penis, obviously. As a doctor, I knew scientific studies disproved the common belief that women tolerated pain better than men did, even if Tara contradicted those studies by failing to pass out at the peak of pain, as I had done. Perhaps I was just a wimp.

Whatever the case, visions of her suffering will be something I will never forget. The injections I gave her provided such little relief that I had to wonder if adding pain was part of creating what Rodney's people considered a delicacy. If that were true, they wouldn't differ much from some humans who inflict pain to increase their sexual pleasure.

The good news was that Tara's pain had been relatively brief.

Not as brief as it had been for me, because I passed out, but it subsided to tolerable levels within a matter of minutes.

The bad news was that eliminating fossil fuels tycoons only marginally increased the length of viable life on Earth. My theory for that was that being a successful politician, maintaining a think tank, or founding a television network all took a significant amount of talent, whereas running a coal mine or an oil field required more luck and greed than talent. Consequently, someone of similar abilities usually replaced whomever we deported. If there was one thing the world didn't have a shortage of, it was people who would do anything for money.

After the final external body part extraction, Rodney agreed to a break, allowing Tara to sleep for several hours. When she awoke, she insisted we go on a run to test her refurbished replacements against Clarice's speed. I was thankful we lived in a remote location. Otherwise, someone surely would have filmed our run and posted it on social media, creating yet another problem for us to deal with. As Tara's test proved, I now had a girlfriend who could win a gold medal in most track and field Olympic events, even if she were competing against the men.

Despite our extraordinary abilities, we still felt helpless. We would be moving on to internal organs next—and that was terrifying. Aside from the pain we would have to endure, what about rejection? All the physical strength in the world wouldn't mean a thing if our bodies rejected a kidney, a liver, or a heart.

Early on Sunday evening, Tara and I were in the kitchen, finishing the last of the ice cream, when Rodney popped back into our heads. Since the couch was kind of gross to sit on at that moment, we stayed at the kitchen table.

"Congratulations!" he said. "Between the two of you, you have added 142 years of viable life to your planet."

I pushed out my jaw and said, "I think we've done enough."

"I agree. But my supervisor will order Earth to be recycled if you don't extend life by at least two hundred years."

"That's ridiculous!" Tara screamed. "At some point, your projections must lose their accuracy. After all, you have to leave room for future conservation measures and technological advances."

"I am sorry," Rodney said. "I do not make the rules."

I took a deep breath to calm my frustration. "What about the time travel possibility you mentioned? I assume that whenever and wherever you would send Tara and me would be important enough to add many years of viable life to our planet. Considering the foodie fetish we aren't supposed to mention, I'm wondering if your people have a conflict of interest. You say your people are ethical. If that's the case, saving Earth must take precedence over indulging your elite."

Rodney cringed. *"Shhh! Shhh!* Stop it! You are going to get me fired. Let me think. . . . Okay, I am going to put together a proposal for my supervisor and plead your case. Maybe we are already close enough to go directly to the time travel mission. If not, I will fight for a maximum of two carefully planned deportations that will only cost something easily replaced, like your livers. For now, just relax and enjoy your evening. I will return tomorrow with a verdict."

He vanished.

* * *

Tara and I used the rest of our evening to stop by the apartment above her storefront to pick up some clothing that better fit her new, slightly taller body. That she walked dogs for a living had previously given her a fit physique. Nevertheless, I looked forward to the day when I could explore every inch of her refurbished legs without the distraction of a full-time planetary consultant, third class, lurking around inside my head. If there was such a thing as perfection, her new legs were it.

After collecting what she needed, Tara walked downstairs to write out a new schedule for her employees, an apology note for her absence, and checks that included advance pay for the coming two weeks, plus a bonus.

Our next stop was a big-box store that was open late. There, Tara picked up several pairs of pants and shoes. Whether her feet were actually bigger than they were before was subject to debate. But as she said, "New feet deserve new shoes."

We concluded our evening out with a stop at a grocery store, where we stocked up on cleaning supplies, food for easy-to-prepare meals, and more beer and ice cream than we normally buy.

Upon returning to the cabin, we took advantage of our enhanced vision to go on another run with Clarice. I didn't have to be a dog-mind-reader to know she thought being able to play with humans who could keep up with her was the absolute best. Well, that, and realizing her agility and quick reflexes still gave her a slight edge in her favorite game of stick-keep-away.

That night, Rodney appeared to be messing with my dreams, because I traveled back in time to places I had obviously never visited before. One such place was Spain during the Spanish Inquisition, another was Salem during the witch trials, and yet another was a plantation in the South during slavery.

At breakfast, I told Tara about my dreams, and she responded by saying, "Oh, he was definitely messing with my dreams too, because I traveled to South America, where a missionary was abusing tribal members; to Canada, where a minister was whipping a native child at a school; and to someplace else I couldn't pinpoint, where a Catholic priest was molesting a young boy."

I tilted my head and replied, "It seems as if we have a common theme."

We were still sitting at the kitchen table, finishing our coffees, when Rodney popped back into our brains. "Knock! Knock!" he said with a wide smile. "Are you ready for the big reveal?"

Chapter 15

The Big Reveal

"The big reveal?" I asked. "Does it have anything to do with the dreams we both had last night?"

"Mayyy-be," he said playfully.

"Please tell us," said Tara.

"I had a talk with my supervisor, as I promised I would. That meeting went much better than expected. Not only did she accept my proposal, but she also promoted me! I am now a full-time planetary consultant, second class."

"Yippee," I snarked.

"Congratulations," Tara said with more sincerity. "What does that mean for all of us?"

"For you, it means your livers and skin will be the last body parts you will have to exchange. After that, you will move directly to time travel. For me, other than a little more status and a little more pay, it means that I have additional flexibility in what I can say to you without oversight—including the big reveal."

"If your big reveal means that you've been lying to us the entire time, I'm going to . . . well, I guess we've pretty much established that Tara and I don't have a lot of recourse. Still, we will be very disappointed in you."

"And you wouldn't want us to be disappointed in you. Would you?" Tara added in a motherly voice.

Rodney bowed his head. "No. I want you to be proud of me. I have always done my best to be truthful with you. Admittedly, there have been instances where either my training or my supervisor has forbidden me from telling you the whole truth, but now that I have the authority to tell you more, I am going to do so."

I poured another round of coffees, took a sip of mine, and warmed my hands around my mug. "Okay, Mister Full-time Planetary Consultant, Second Class, we're listening."

"Remember when we first met, and I mentioned an unfortunate incident that resulted in my people being forbidden from physically traveling to your planet?"

"Sure," I said.

"Well, early in what you call *biblical times*, we disguised ourselves in various forms and made frequent in-person visits. Those visits had nothing to do with the environmental problems that concern us now. We just wanted to nudge Earth-humans onto a path of peace, love, and generosity. Once we accomplished that, our plan was to get out of there and let humanity develop on its own."

Rodney unfolded his virtual chair and sat down. "Unfortunately, the humans during that era were less ready than my people expected them to be. It was a terrible miscalculation on our part. Because of their primitive nature, those humans considered us gods, and multiple religions sprouted up to worship us. The worshipping was not so bad. After all, who doesn't like that kind of attention?"

He rocked back before continuing. "Then we observed humans using their religion like a club to justify their selfish and violent desires. Even after some well-intentioned humans authored religious documents to provide stable guidance, those documents, which became books in the Bible, were perverted—first through self-serving translations and later through wild interpretations."

"How do you mean?" Tara asked.

"Here's an example I think you will appreciate. Go onto the internet and enter a search for 'Numbers 5: 11-31.'"

Tara hurried into the living room to retrieve her smartphone. She stood for a moment as she typed, then slowly walked back to the kitchen table. "Got it."

"Select the New International Version if you can, since that version features scholarly translations from the oldest Aramaic, Greek, and Hebrew texts available and is not just a modern rehash of the King James Version."

I leaned over to follow along as she read.

"Oh, my God!" Tara exclaimed. "This is the most misogynistic thing I've ever seen!"

"Keep going."

When she finished, she said, "Holy shit! It lays out a crude process for inducing abortions. One that wouldn't work, of course, but the intent is still there."

"Exactly. Back then, humans did not call it abortion, but the New International Version leaves no doubt about the intent by using the word *miscarry*. Including permission to end a pregnancy, not the misogyny, in the original texts was something we encouraged as a way to prevent a future population explosion and to make every child a wanted child. Knowing that, think about how many Christian denominations oppose abortion. The leaders of those denominations are obviously aware of what is in the Book of Numbers, yet they choose to ignore the lesson we tried to teach those early humans. Can you guess why that is?"

"Because they're also aware that the abortion issue gains them money and power," Tara said.

"Precisely!" Rodney replied.

"So are your people essentially an amalgamate of what humans call God?" I asked.

"Perhaps. But obviously we are not gods. Hey, I just got a promotion. What kind of god needs a promotion? If your planet survives, someday your people may be able to do what my people can do. We just had a multi-million-year head start on you—that is all."

Clarice leaned against my chair, and I scratched her behind the ears as I considered all that Rodney had revealed. "Okay. Assume I buy that. What does any of that have to do with saving the Earth from climate change, exchanging original body parts for refurbished ones, and engaging in time travel missions?"

"Not every goal is singular. And now that I have my promotion, I can explain it all to you more freely. First, my people really do want to save your planet. In fact, since so many conservative Christians are in cahoots with climate-change-denying political leaders and fossil fuels corporations, we feel responsible for planting the seed that led to that. A successful time travel mission will help to break up that cozy threesome. The body parts exchange also has multiple purposes. Yes, the elite of my people really do eat what we take, but as I mentioned before, we justify that the same way Earth-humans justify eating whale meat. And since satisfying the epicurean desires of our elite produces the financial support necessary for planet-saving programs like this one, it is easier for consultants like me to look the other way too. More importantly, however, is that your new, superior refurbished parts will help to keep you alive when you time travel."

"What about the skin you said we must exchange?" Tara asked. "Requiring us to have refurbished skin makes me wonder if we're gonna have to arrive nude, like in the *Terminator* movies."

Rodney smiled. "Yeah, as part of researching your planet, I watched all the *Terminator* movies—something I could do in less than a minute of your time. I can see why you might associate changing your skin with arriving nude. Do not worry. You can travel to wherever I send you fully clothed."

"That's a relief," Tara said.

"The real reason for the skin exchange is twofold. First, our elite foodie sponsors consider human skin—and human livers for that matter—to be the ultimate delicacies. Without those items in return, our funding would dry up. The second reason is more practical. And for this one, you may want to brace yourself."

"We're as braced as we'll ever be," I said.

"My people left your planet after what you would consider to be the Old Testament Era. That we had miscalculated the readiness of Earth-humans to move beyond their primitive nature so frustrated our supreme supervisor that she called a meeting of all the top planetary consultants. It was at that meeting when one of our finest consultants suggested a second-chance plan that received the supreme supervisor's blessing. He would return to Earth to occupy a human brain. It would not be a short-term intergalactic occupation, like I am doing with both of your brains now. Instead, it would be a physical occupation that began at childhood, allowing the consultant to obtain a more accurate and long-term understanding of the humans around him."

"Jesus Christ!" I exclaimed. "You're not saying—"

"Yes. Him. At first, the plan worked exactly as we had hoped it would. Our new consultant-occupied human was able to form relationships as a child and later use his advanced knowledge to perform what the primitive population on Earth believed to be miracles. By the time he was thirty, he was drawing sizeable crowds and using his great influence to deliver our guiding message of peace, love, and generosity."

"Oh, I can hardly wait for the *but*," I said.

"But something went wrong. Our consultant occupying the body of Jesus never returned after the crucifixion event. The pain

91

of experiencing death on a cross made him hate the human race so much that he went rogue and has been jumping from body to body doing evil in the name of Christianity ever since.

"The news that one of our own was engaging in such deplorable conduct took many Earth-years to reach our supreme supervisor, but when she found out she immediately banned all in-person visits to your planet and ordered the retrieval of our consultant. Unfortunately, all retrieval attempts via deportation have failed, because each time our consultant was able to feel the pull and expel himself from the body at the last moment.

"Sometimes he hides in obscure humans. Other times he hides out in the open, almost daring us to make a retrieval attempt. Occupying Adolf Hitler was one of the times our consultant dared us. Once, at a Christmas celebration, he said, 'The work that Christ started but could not finish, I—Adolf Hitler—will conclude.' And that was just one of many similar statements he gave in speeches or in writing. It is also the real reason my supervisor refused to let you deport Adolf Hitler. We had already done it.

"While Hitler's deportation failed to capture our consultant, at least it provided us with a valuable learning experience. Only after that failure did we realize that replacing deported bodies with inanimate replicas suitable for Earth's burial rituals was necessary, and that deporting someone too late in life was a mistake, when we could have done it earlier and created positive change. But it does explain for you why Hitler's body was never found.

"Another time our consultant dared us occurred when he, as Donald Trump, bragged in front of reporters that he was 'The Chosen One.' Unfortunately, even Tara's creative idea of deporting Fred Trump still allowed our consultant to slip from our grasp."

I nodded in understanding. "So, obviously, you're sending us on a time travel mission to catch this consultant."

"What's this consultant's name?" Tara asked.

"Just call him *Ralph*. It is the closest translation from my language."

"And what does this have to do with our skin?" I asked.

"Your new, specially refurbished skin will provide both a repellent and a barrier to prevent Ralph from entering your body. After all, if he gets inside your brain, you will be just another puppet for him to manipulate."

"For how long will our skin protect us?" I asked.

"Since all human skin renews itself over time, your protection won't last forever. I will monitor your skin health when you time travel and warn you if waning protection ever becomes an issue."

"Okay," Tara said. "But if *you* can't capture Ralph, how the hell are we supposed to capture him?"

"I will provide you with some trap-capsules that will, hopefully, prevent him from switching bodies long enough for me to grab him. Just jam one in any orifice of any body Ralph is occupying, and I will do the rest."

"Where will you be sending us?" Tara asked.

"Your dreams last night gave you a hint of that. Your world has more than its share of evil people, but since doing evil in the name of Christianity is how Ralph gets his revenge, we can limit our search to people involved in events that fit his goals. I will send you backward in time sequentially. That way, if you are unsuccessful, earlier versions of Ralph will not suspect you are coming."

"What about language?" I asked. "Undoubtedly, we will need to speak more than just English."

"I will be with you the entire time. When someone speaks in a foreign language, I will take over your auditory system, so you will hear the words in English. And when you speak, I will take over your vocal system, so your words will come out in the

93

appropriate language. The process will feel strange at first, but you will get used to it."

"If, by some miracle, Tara and I are successful in helping you capture Ralph, can you promise us that there will be no more surprises and that you will finally let us go back to our normal lives?"

"You have my word, Stefan, even if I have to go to my supervisor's supervisor to get it done. Livers, skin, and Ralph, that is it. Your new livers, by the way, will allow either of you to drink anyone you need to under the table. It could be the most undervalued of your new superpowers. Do not forget you have it. Now, whom shall we deport next?"

Chapter 16

Meanwhile, We Do Have Lives

After assurances from Rodney that the technicians in the refurb department designed all body parts, including internal organs, to be rejection-proof, we got to work on whom to select for our final deportations. For those, I chose a youthful version of Senator Mitch McConnell, and Tara chose conspiracy theorist Alex Jones. If you're wondering why she didn't select any of the well-qualified conspiracy theorists and climate change deniers with shows on Fox News, remember that she had put most of them out of work when she designated Rupert Murdoch for deportation.

Since we had just enough fentanyl left for one dose for each of us, we combined the liver sacrifices and skin exchanges into a single process. I went first, followed by Tara. Despite Rodney's warning about the additional pain involved with changing my skin, I passed out as usual and didn't notice a difference. This time Tara passed out too, so while the shock was obviously worse for her, the duration was shorter.

Once we had sufficiently recovered, I called out from the

couch, "Hey, Rodney. How come we didn't get to deport anyone for exchanging our skin?"

He popped back into view and replied, "Oh, did you want to do that?"

"Not necessarily. But I think we should both get sacrifice credits for use later if more deportations become necessary."

"Hold on." He blinked out and back. "Done! Your accounts now show one sacrifice credit each."

"What's the total count of the livable years we've added to the planet?" Tara asked from the cushion next to me.

"Alex Jones produced only a minor effect, because the people who paid attention to him and his Infowars show and website were already so far out there and unreachable that they just migrated to another far-right celebrity whack job. Mitch McConnell, on the other hand, was one of your most effective deportations. Human rights, funding for education, help for the poor, making the rich pay their fair share, and many other issues improved without him there to block progress. The issue your sacrifice was intended for—adding life to your planet—came out even better in my post sacrifice simulations than those I conducted beforehand. All in all, my projections now show that we have added 156 years of viable life to Planet Earth. A big congratulations to both of you!"

"Now that the dread of sacrifices is behind us, I'm kind of looking forward to a little time travel," I said.

"Me too," added Tara.

"Do not get too giddy," Rodney warned. "Even though you have both experienced extreme pain, your lives were always safe. Now danger will replace that pain. I will be with you when you time travel, just like I am now, but I cannot instantly pull you back to present time whenever you ask. You could actually die out there."

"Why can't you pull us back?" Tara asked.

"Because of a treaty signed at The Intergalactic Time Travel Symposium."

"TITTS?" I asked.

Rodney snorted. "I never thought of it that way, but yes. TITTS was a gathering of all known time-travel-capable species to study ways to limit abuse. It was too easy for anyone to time jump onto a competitor's planet, sabotage something, and jump right back out. To prevent that from happening, every affected species signed a treaty requiring a three-day stay."

"Did TITTS participants agree on a standard length of day?" I asked.

"No. They go by the length of day on the planet where the time travel occurs."

"Do any species ever cheat on the TITTS treaty?" Tara asked.

"No. Because the other treaty signers would interpret that as an act of war."

"Where are we time traveling to first?" I asked.

"That is something I am working on now. Ralph can move from body to body at will, but he cannot time travel. Therefore, we are going to start with suspects in recent history and work our way back, if necessary. Unfortunately, I do not have a way of detecting where Ralph is at any point in time. You may end up jamming body-switching-prevention trap-capsules into the orifices of quite a few unoccupied people as we try to catch him."

I couldn't help smiling when I asked, "What do we say to anyone we wrongfully accuse? Thrusting a capsule up someone's nose—or worse—is just a wee bit personal."

"I would not worry about that. You will not be encountering anyone you would like to be friends with."

Clarice jumped onto my lap and rolled over for a belly rub. As she moaned her approval of my scratching in just the right spot, I considered the effect Tara's and my time travels could have on those who depended on us. "Hey, Rodney. What about Clarice and our jobs? Saving the world doesn't eliminate our other responsibilities. We simply can't disappear for days on end, as we time travel to who knows where."

"That is one of the beauties of time travel," he said. "You could disappear for ten years and still return to your cabin one second after you left."

"Ten years!" Tara exclaimed. "What about aging?"

"You will age normally while time traveling. Do not worry about returning with wrinkles, however, as I fully expect each mission to last precisely three days. If you stay out of trouble, the worst thing you will return with is a variety of parasites from the lack of sanitation. For those, either Stefan can prescribe some pills or I can switch out the infested organ."

I moved from the couch to the kitchen table, where I had a pad of paper. I started making a list as I said, "You say you're still working on where to send us, but one of the dreams you sent to Tara took place in South America, and I assume other tropical locations could be on our agenda too. Therefore, before we go, I'd like to make sure Tara and I are fully vaccinated for hepatitis, tetanus, diphtheria, meningitis, typhoid, and yellow fever. I would also like to pick up some chloroquine pills for malaria. Despite what you say, there are many things we can catch that switching out an organ can't cure. This nonstop pace has also screwed up our lives. We both have bills to pay and really need to at least make an appearance at our places of work."

"I need at least a week," Tara said.

"And our vaccinations will need at least two weeks to become effective," I added.

"I do not know," Rodney said hesitantly.

"Oh, come on," Tara begged. "You said time is different for you.

Just think how much better prepared Stefan and I will be once we've rested up and have had two weeks to become acclimated to our body parts."

"My planetary consultant training was very specific on this issue. Brief breaks lead to success. Long breaks lead to second thoughts."

Tara switched to her motherly voice. "But Rodney, you're now a full-time planetary consultant, second class. You have advanced beyond your training, and you know Stefan and me. If we were gonna back out, we would've done so a long time ago. Two weeks is all we're asking."

He took a deep virtual breath. "Okay. Be ready in exactly two weeks. I will have a high probability target ready for you."

He vanished.

* * *

The following day, I headed back to work for the first time since I had left a voice mail message for my head nurse, Sharon, to tell her I was quarantining after a positive COVID-19 test. But that was in a timeline prior to deporting Fred Trump, Ronald Reagan, and others. Was my absence excuse still valid?

"Good morning, Doctor Westin!" said Jennifer, the receptionist, as I entered the hospital. "How was Bonaire?"

Oh, that sucked! Memories of Tara's and my vacation on the Caribbean island began to materialize in my brain. Apparently, we had a great time. "Just wonderful, Jennifer. Thank you for asking."

I stepped into the elevator and texted Tara: *In this timeline, we just returned from a vacation in Bonaire.*

Thanx 4 the heads up! she texted back.

When I reached my office, Sharon was waiting for me. "How was your vaca—" She stopped, looked me up and down and smiled. "When most people vacation in the Caribbean, they come back tanner. You came back taller!"

"Really? It must be the joys of new shoes and strong sunscreen."

"So how was it?"

"Friendly people, warm tropical breezes, and stunning sunsets. How can anything beat that?"

I hung up my coat and walked down the hall to get a cup of coffee. Along the way, various hospital staff welcomed me back—most displaying perplexed expressions as they tried to figure out what was different about me. Despite the unfairness of my Bonaire vacation being only a memory, at least the passage of time was enough to put doubt in people's minds about my increased height.

As I returned from the medical staff lounge, I stood for a moment and just listened. The hospital sounded so . . . normal. The hallway looked normal too, with no sick patients on beds, waiting to be wheeled in when a room opened up. I looked at my patient schedule and didn't see a single COVID-19 case. Was the pandemic already on the downswing? Had it ended? Did it never exist? Memories of what happened, if I had them, had yet to surface. Instead, all of my appointments were for minor surgeries or follow-ups on previous surgeries. Never had *routine* felt so exhilarating!

Seeing with my own eyes the good Tara and I had accomplished was so much better than hearing it from Rodney or reading about it on the internet. At that moment, all the doubts I'd had about whether the two of us were doing the right thing melted away.

* * *

For the first time since we had become a couple, my workday ended sooner than Tara's did. I returned to the cabin and arranged all her vaccines on the kitchen table while I waited. When she finally walked through the door, I asked, "Tough day at the outside office?"

"You doctors, with your nurses and secretaries, have it easy!" she grumbled. "Try being a sole proprietor for a day. First, I had to pay all the bills; then I had to update my books; then I had to talk an employee out of quitting; then I had to clean the bathroom and sweep the floors; then I had to apologize to an unhappy customer even though he was wrong; and finally, when I got outside to actually walk some dogs, one slipped his collar and took off into the mountains."

"Oh, no! Did you get him back?"

She smiled. "That was the one highlight of my day. I secured the other dogs to a tree and raced after the escapee. Despite his head start, I chased him down and had him under control in a matter of minutes. I don't know who was more stunned by how fast I could move—me or the dog. These new legs are gonna come in handy!"

I pointed to the syringes and vaccine vials on the table and said, "Pull down your pants."

She looked at me with wide eyes and said, "I don't think that's where the shots are supposed to go."

"I know."

* * *

Our fourteen-day vacation from Rodney passed way too quickly. Still, there were many things to appreciate: Multiple dinners with Amy (I finally took her up on her race challenge and let her beat me by a step). A racquetball match with Bruce, a physician friend from the hospital (after losing to him for years, I finally kicked his ass). Sliding under the cabin to replace a leaky pipe (I didn't have to worry about a flashlight or that the space was too tight to apply enough torque to my wrench). And the list went on.

Then, early on the fifteenth day, while Tara, Clarice, and I were in bed, enjoying a lazy snuggle: "Knock! Knock! Let's get going, humans! There is no time like the past."

Ah, fucking Rodney!

Chapter 17

An Introduction to Time Travel

I sat up in bed, taking in the image of Rodney, wearing heavy makeup, a wild pink wig, and a tight glittery dress. "Why are you dressed like that?"

He fluffed up his hair and said, "I will give you a hint. It has to do with our first target."

"We're going after a drag queen?" I asked.

"No!" he said with a disappointed expression. "Fred Phelps."

"I don't know who he is."

"Haven't you heard of the Westboro Baptist Church?"

Tara slid out from under the covers and swung her feet onto the floor. "Oh! They're the *God Hates Fags* people!"

"Yes!" he exclaimed. "And Fred Phelps was the church's founder. He died in 2014, at the age of eighty-four. You will be visiting him on April 21, 2013 in Medford, Massachusetts. That was the day before members of the Westboro Baptist Church had intended to disrupt the funeral of Krystle Campbell, who was killed in the Boston Marathon bombing. They ultimately chickened out, when teamsters and a motorcycle club showed up to block access to the funeral. Fred would not have actively participated, anyway. He was only traveling with the group so he could direct the disruption from a rundown motel at the edge of town."

Tara shot me a puzzled look before saying to Rodney, "I thought Ralph was in Donald Trump at that time. Can he occupy more than one body at once?"

"No. But he has the ability to move so quickly between bodies that sometimes it seems as if he can. That is why Ralph will probably be difficult to track down. Working in our favor is that my research suggests that Ralph sticks with one primary person throughout the most malevolent years of that person's life. The only known exceptions are when he temporarily leaves his primary subject to control a nearby body for his immediate benefit or when he takes on a part-time side project to relieve boredom. Fred Phelps was almost certainly one of those side projects. Also, keep in mind that we are now in a new timeline, where Donald Trump never existed. While Trump was Ralph's primary subject in the original timeline, this new Trumpless timeline only increases the probability that Ralph occupied Fred Phelps as either a side project or his primary subject. And if he ever occupied Fred, Krystle Campbell's funeral would have been an irresistible final opportunity to do something disgusting."

"At least this doesn't sound like it will be a dangerous mission," I said. "We can easily handle a man in his eighties, even without our enhanced body parts."

"Do not underestimate any person or any situation," Rodney said in a stern voice. "It could get you killed. Realistically, however, I believe this will serve as a relatively gentle introduction to time travel."

I got out of bed and padded into the kitchen to start up a pot of coffee. "Rodney, what's all this money doing on the table?"

"That is for you and Tara to divide up and stuff into your pockets. And next to the money are your IDs. The TITTS treaty prevents me from sending you with any weapons or luggage. The clothing you wear, plus money, IDs, and personal items that fit into your pockets are all you can bring. If capturing Ralph requires more than one time jump, I will continue to provide you with money and IDs that correspond to the time and location. For this first jump, your own casual pants and shirts will be sufficient. If we go back further in time, I will also provide you with clothing that corresponds to the time and location."

Tara joined me in the kitchen. "Who knew time travel would be so complicated?"

I chuckled.

"That's not what I meant," she said. "I was talking about all the rules and preparations, not the actual traveling."

"I know."

"On the bright side, maybe I'll get some cool vintage shoes and dresses out of this." She looked up. "Rodney, I hope you have good taste in clothing!"

He smiled, held out his arms, and twirled. "This fabulous dress should tell you all you need to know about my impeccable fashion sense!" His cheerful expression grew serious. "Please eat your breakfast, take a shower, walk Clarice, and anything else you need to do. Be ready to time jump in two hours." He vanished.

*　*　*

We materialized next to the dumpster behind the Happy Riser Motel, on Sunday, April 21, 2013.

"Yuck!" Tara said as she scanned the immediate scenery of an overflowing dumpster and a stained cement pad littered with broken glass. "It smells like the hog barn at a county fair."

"Rodney, we've arrived," I announced.

"I know. I am still with you. To limit distractions on time travel missions, I will generally keep my visual image turned off. Please check into the motel."

"Do we actually have to stay here?" Tara asked.

"Yes. Fred Phelps, and everyone he is traveling with, will be arriving here this evening."

"Brrr!" I said. "We're not dressed for this. Rodney, can you please let us know what the weather will be like before departing on time jumps from now on?"

"I have placed a notation in your account," he said.

We walked around to the front of the single-story building, entered the tiny reception area, and rang the bell. A moment passed before a gaunt man wearing a sweat-stained T-shirt entered from the back office and approached the counter.

"Hi," I said. "We'd like a room with a king-sized bed."

"Full-sized only," he replied.

"Do you have a room with two beds?" I asked.

"Yes."

"We'll take that. On the far end, if possible."

He pointed to a sign behind his shoulder and said, "Check-in is at three."

I glanced at the clock behind his other shoulder. "It's already a few minutes after two."

"Come back in an hour. I'll have a room for you then."

We stepped into the parking lot and shivered.

I called out, "Rodney, do you have access to a map?"

"Yes."

"See if you can find someplace within walking distance where we can buy coats."

"There is an Army-Navy surplus store to your right. Two blocks away."

"That will have to do."

Tara laughed as she proclaimed, "Rodney: Earth's first living GPS."

* * *

106

We returned to the motel an hour later, wearing matching blue peacoats and floppy wide-brimmed hats. I suspected our new outerwear made us look like we were trying too hard to blend in. Even so, I liked my coat more than I thought I would. Perhaps Tara had the right idea about using Rodney to improve our wardrobes.

This time, we were able to check in. Obviously—and I say this dripping with sarcasm—the motel had used the extra time to make sure our room was thoroughly cleaned. At least when I inspected between the mattresses and box springs I saw no signs of bedbugs.

My complaining aside, getting the end room I had requested turned out to be just what we needed. Since the motel had an L-shaped configuration, we could look out our window and, with a bit of effort, see people coming and going from all the other rooms.

"There they are," said Tara.

We watched as the slender, balding Fred Phelps and his group moved into three side-by-side rooms, almost directly opposite us. They would be easy to keep track of.

I reached into my pocket, pulled out one of the trap-capsules Rodney had given me, and rolled it between my fingers. "What do we do now? I don't think we can simply knock on the door and jam a capsule up Fred's nose when he answers."

"What would a doctor do?" Rodney asked.

We sat in silence, peering out our motel room window as we thought.

"I've got it!" I said.

* * *

After two hours of watching, I sighed in frustration. "Is he ever going to leave his room?"

107

After another hour, Tara asked, "Rodney, can you look into the past and give us a time?"

"I am sorry," he said. "My people do not have the ability to time travel in that manner."

Fifty minutes later, I stood and said, "Finally! But where would Fred and that other man be going this late in the evening, a strip club?"

I hurried out the door, walking across the parking lot, as if heading for the reception area. I picked up my pace to make sure I was near Fred when he opened the passenger side door of his rental car.

"Stefan!" Tara yelled from the door of our room. "Ask for some toilet paper too!"

"What?" I shouted as I turned back toward her—and nailed Fred in the nose with my elbow.

I reached out and caught Fred before he hit the ground. "I'm so sorry! I didn't see you. Are you okay?"

He looked at me with his hand covering his nose. Blood seeped down onto his lips. "Watch where you're going! I think you broke my nose."

"Oh! I'm so, so sorry. I'm a doctor." I tilted my head and offered him my well-practiced expression of concern. "Lower your hand so I can have a look."

As Fred tentatively lowered his hand, his chubby companion stepped around from the opposite side of the car to observe.

I squinted and said, "Your nose looks broken to me, but it's hard to tell for sure in this light. Let's get you into your room, where I can see it better."

The chubby man and I each grasped an arm and gently led Fred to his room. There we helped him to the foot of the bed, where he sat for his examination.

"What happened?" asked a bun-haired woman who was already in the room.

"This man hit him in the nose," said the chubby man.

"It was an accident," I said in a sincere voice. "Fortunately, I'm a doctor, and I see noses like this often." I sopped up some blood with a tissue and put on a show of carefully examining Fred's nose. "It looks like the bridge is dislocated. I can straighten your nose right now, before it swells too much. Or, if you're squeamish about such things, I recommend a trip to the hospital emergency room."

Fred looked at me with a relieved expression. "You can fix it now?"

"Yes. And if you put some ice on it immediately afterward, it'll be as good as new in a few days."

"How bad is this going to hurt?"

"The pain will probably make your eyes water, but it'll only last for the few seconds I take to set your nose. After that, you'll experience some minor discomfort for a week or so, which you can limit with some ibuprofen."

He took a deep breath and said, "Let's get this over with."

"Lie back."

As Fred followed my instructions, I surreptitiously reached into my pocket and palmed a trap-capsule. Then I leaned down, positioned my hands on each side of his face—and his eyes rolled back into his head.

The chubby man nailed me in the ear with a Gideon's Bible!

I crashed to the floor, dropping the trap-capsule when I landed on my elbow.

The chubby man glared down at me with his arm cocked, ready to hit me again. "Nice try. I was wondering when my people were going to send someone after me." He reached behind him and turned the deadbolt. "If you're going to shove something up my nose to keep me in place, you're going to have to be sneakier than that." He flung the Bible—hitting me in the arm—and picked up a lamp.

Wood splintered from the doorframe!

The door crashed against the wall, and Tara stepped inside. She paused to admire the damage from her kick. "That was *sooo* cool!"

The chubby man looked from Tara to me and back.

She reached out a hand. "Hi! I'm Tara. You must be Ralph."

The chubby man set down the lamp and scowled. "At least have the decency to call me Jesus."

"No. I like Ralph," she said.

I ran my hand along the filthy carpet, found the trap-capsule, and stuffed it into my pocket as I stood.

Ralph shot me a disgusted look. "Is this the first time we've met?"

"Yes," I said.

"Then I assume we will be doing this again sometime in the past."

"Perhaps."

"Next time come see me when I'm not occupying an old man." He looked down at his extended belly. "Or someone tubby."

He turned his head toward Tara. "A rematch in Salem, perhaps? You have one hell of a kick, but kicking won't do you any good if you're swinging from a noose." He smiled as he raised a hand and waved with just his fingers. "Toodle-oo!"

The chubby man collapsed. Tara caught him and eased him onto the bed.

Fred Phelps sat up and began praying. I gently pushed him back down and snapped his nose into place. "Remember—ice and ibuprofen." I pulled three hundred dollars from my pocket and set the money on the end table. "That's for the door."

As soon as we stepped outside, Tara spun and kicked high into the air, shouting, "Who's the superhero now, Doctor Refurb?"

I laughed as we walked across the parking lot and returned to our room. There I stood for a moment before saying, "Is there any reason we need to stay here tonight? The police will probably show up, and I'd much rather spend the next three nights in a nice hotel than here or in a jail cell."

"No," Rodney said.

"Then let's pack up our luggage and go."

"We don't have any luggage," said Tara.

"All the better."

Even though our first time travel mission hadn't accomplished our goal, we learned from the experience. Other than understanding just how slippery Ralph could be, we also picked up on the fact that Rodney had overestimated how much money two people would go through in three days. Most of the bills he'd given us were hundreds, allowing us to rent a suite at an upscale hotel and enjoy meals that would satisfy most foodies. Spending all our money was hard work, but we were penniless when we returned to present time.

Chapter 18

Rookie Mistakes

W e arrived back at the cabin with Clarice still standing in the exact spot she was when we left her. That we had blinked out wearing lightweight clothes and blinked back in wearing matching blue peacoats and floppy wide-brimmed hats unfazed her. Apparently, when you're a dog accustomed to humans who magically turn on lights upon entering rooms, produce food without a hunt, and give rides in metal boxes with no visible means of propulsion, a simple instant wardrobe change doesn't even register on the "They Must Be Gods" meter.

After we had a few minutes to change clothes and settle back in, I poured myself the last of the coffee from the still-warm pot and asked, "Rodney, am I correct in assuming that we are going directly to Salem?"

He materialized and replied, "No. Because if we find Ralph there, and he escapes, we will lose the opportunity to catch him closer to present time."

Tara joined me in the kitchen. "Why is that?" she asked, before reaching across the table to steal my coffee mug.

"Technically, there is no difference in effort to jump five

hundred years back in time than there is to jump five years back in time," he said. "But to assure that Ralph will not be expecting you, I must schedule each successive jump to an earlier period, while at the same time being careful not to send you so far back that we eliminate a prime opportunity for capture that is more recent. Scheduling this way is doubly important, since the further I send you back, the greater the magnification of unintended changes to the current timeline. For example, what if you and Stefan do something that prevents the meeting of two people who were supposed to have children together? Doing so five hundred years into the past could produce significantly different results than doing it only five years into the past."

"So where are we going to next?" I asked.

Rodney snapped his fingers and a safari hat, quick-dry shirt, and khaki pants replaced his hoodie and jeans. "To the Amazon Rainforest of Brazil, to seek the Reverend Wesley Wilson, a missionary who had been abusing a tribe there in the 1950s."

I tugged my mug from Tara's hands and asked, "Don't missionaries have a long sordid history of abusing South American tribes?"

"Yes," he said. "Much more than the public is aware of."

"What made Wesley Wilson different?" I asked.

"On the surface—nothing. Like so many other missionaries, he forced Christianity onto people he thought to be primitive and in need of being 'saved.' The process typically starts with the simple sharing of the 'good news,' proceeds to getting the tribe dependent on the missionary for food, shelter, and clothing, which leads to the withholding of those items if Christian compliance is not achieved, and, for some, it concludes with sexual abuse under the guise of expelling demons from their souls. What differentiated Wesley from other abusive missionaries was that he ultimately took his ministry one step further and convinced the tribe that he was Jesus's only male cousin, and therefore a god himself."

"And Ralph enjoyed pretending to be a god," Tara surmised.

"Exactly!"

I reached behind me and grabbed the bottle of chloroquine off the counter. "If we're traveling to the Amazon Rainforest, I must ask for a delay. We need to take one chloroquine pill a week for malaria, beginning two weeks before travel."

"Oh, that is not a problem," Rodney said. "Each of you grasp two pills and a glass of water."

We did what he asked.

"One moment. . . ." He flashed out and back before dramatically flicking out his right arm and shouting, "Ta-da! It is now two weeks earlier."

Tara and I looked across to the living room, where earlier versions of us were snuggled up on the couch.

Rodney lifted a finger to his mouth. *"Shhh!* Life will be much less confusing if they do not know you are here. Just quietly swallow one pill each."

We did as he said.

He dramatically flicked out his right arm again and shouted, "Ta-da! It is now one week earlier."

This time, Tara and I had landed in our own laps. We looked at our duplicates with our mouths wide open, and they did the same.

"Oops! I can fix that!" Rodney flicked out his arm again and shouted, "Ta-da!"

We landed in the top row of the Washington-Grizzly Stadium in Missoula. Sleet was falling, and the University of Montana football team had the ball.

I perused Tara, in her black sports bra and leggings, and said, "You seem a bit underdressed for today's game."

"Yeah, but now that we're here, I wanna see if they score."

We shivered through three plays before the running back fumbled the ball away.

"Oh, thank God," she said. "I don't think I could have made it through a long drive."

"Drink up!" I said.

We swallowed our pills, and just before Rodney spirited us away, Tara stood and yelled, "Go, Griz!"

When we materialized back at the kitchen table, piled up in front of us were hiking boots, socks, shorts, T-shirts, hats, passports, money, and tiny bottles of bug dope and sunscreen.

"Get dressed," Rodney said. "You leave in ten minutes."

Tara closed her eyes for a moment, as if deep in thought. "Wait a minute! Rodney, you told me earlier that we age normally when we time travel. If that's the case, don't we now each have two chloroquine pills dissolving in our stomachs?"

His face grew concerned. "Oh, dear. I suppose you do. That was a rookie mistake on my part. I am sure you will be fine."

"Rodney is right about that," I said. "The primary reason for starting chloroquine two weeks before travel is to allow for a medication adjustment in the event one of us has a reaction. Now that we've lost that adjustment opportunity, what's most important from this point on is that we continue with the medication for four weeks after we return."

"Wait a minute!" Tara said. "Rodney, you also had us time travel three times in quick succession without the required three-day stay. Didn't you just commit an act of war?"

His face grew even more concerned. "Oh, dear. I suppose I did. Double rookie mistake. Hold on!"

He blinked away for what seemed like longer than usual.

"Whew! That was close!" Rodney declared upon his return. "But no worries. I have cleared everything up. Earth has been spared."

"Earth has been spared!" Tara screamed.

"Well, yeah. You were the ones partaking in the forbidden time jumps."

I facepalmed. "Give us fifteen minutes."

Chapter 19

Are You Crazy?

Once we were dressed, I asked Rodney, "What year are we traveling to?"

"Wesley Wilson was with the tribe for nearly twenty years, so I picked 1958, which is shortly after he moved into the sexual molestation stage of his operation and a few years before he declared himself to be Jesus's only male cousin. That way, if I am wrong about Ralph occupying his body, you can at least do something to stop the molestations."

"Okay, we're ready," I said.

Rodney flicked out his arm to send us on our way.

Heat and humidity engulfed Tara and me as we materialized on the muddy bank of a river that was too small to be the Amazon.

I turned slowly, with my eyes darting in all directions. Other than the tea-colored river, dominating my view was a dark-green rainforest canopy that stretched over massive green ferns and pink and yellow flowers of every size and shape. "Where are we?"

"On a tributary of the Rio Negro, some two hundred miles northwest of Manaus," Rodney replied.

"Now what do we do?" Tara asked.

"There should be a path directly behind you. Follow it to the village, a short distance away. Oh, and watch out for venomous snakes and stinging ants."

"Stinging ants?" I asked.

"Yes. Snakes are seldom dangerous unless you step on them. The ants, however, will get angry if you even step in their path. Especially the big black ones your people call bullet ants."

Something roared in the trees!

"Holy shit!" Tara shrieked. "I'm already terrified. I can only imagine what this place will be like at night."

I started down the path, with Tara practically on my heels. "Speaking of night, we have nothing but the clothes on our back. Rodney, where are we supposed to sleep tonight?"

"I am not sure," he said.

Tara's eyes grew wide. "You're not sure?"

"Perhaps you can make some friends," he suggested.

"Oh, great," I added sarcastically. "Maybe the jaguars would like to cuddle."

The path serpentined around some huge kapok trees before reaching the edge of a village that paralleled the river. There, the trees gave way to a clearing with roughly twenty thatch-roofed huts.

We stood quietly just inside the clearing, watching tribal members at work repairing nets and tending to some chickens. When a child spotted us, she called out to the others, and a group of fifteen or so children ran toward us, full of excitement.

Rodney anticipated what was about to happen and said, "Other than the prayers and Bible verses these children recite, they know very little English. When they speak, I will take over your auditory system, so you will hear their words in English. And when you speak, I will take over your vocal system, so your words will come out in their language."

Tara leaned down to greet the children. "Hello, my name is Tara," she said before glancing at me with a silly grin, indicating the weirdness of Rodney manipulating her speech. She turned back to the children and smiled. "Can you take me to your leader?"

"Leader!" I blurted. "You sound like an alien greeting humans in a cheesy sci-fi flick."

Tara looked up. "Rodney! I was trying to say *headman*, not leader."

"Sorry," he said. "I have entered a correction in my notes. It will not happen again."

A boy, who appeared to be about seven, grasped Tara's hand, and he and the rest of the children led us toward the center of the village. I followed behind, doing what came naturally for me—observing the children for signs of disease, malnutrition, or abuse. Although most of the children were thin, none appeared to be unhealthy, and they all wore T-shirts and shorts, which I assumed were hand-me-downs from some church or charity. Then my eyes locked on the children's legs. Several had red welts on the back of their thighs, and when a girl turned to smile at me, I noticed she had a welt across the front of her legs too.

I hurried to catch up to Tara and whispered, "I have a plan. Let me talk first."

She nodded.

The children dropped us off at a large hut, perched atop stilts made from tree trunks. We climbed the stairs and peered through the open doorframe. There, in a hammock, was a svelte, salt-and-pepper-haired white man, reading a Bible. He lowered the book and said slowly, "We don't get many visitors here. Can I help you?"

I strode confidently toward him and thrust out my hand. "Are you Reverend Wesley Wilson?"

"Who wants to know?"

"I'm Doctor Stefan Westin, and this is my nurse, Miss Tara Kramer. We represent the Church of the Sacred Bleeding Heart of Jesus."

He stared at me for a moment before fixing his gaze on Tara. "Never heard of it. Where's it located?"

"In Los Angeles."

"I don't get out that way much."

I chuckled and said, "That's okay. We don't get out your way much either."

He didn't smile.

I continued. "Our calling is to visit Brazilian missions of all Christian denominations to offer medical support. A fisherman dropped us off on his way upriver and is due to pick us up in three days. If you'd be so kind as to introduce us to Reverend Wilson and provide us with shelter for a few days, we'd be very much obliged."

"I am Reverend Wilson." He squinted. "You two are the cleanest people I've seen in years. How'd you manage that?"

"We had a bit of an accident downriver that dumped us and our medical supplies into the water. We came out clean but lost our supplies. We plan to head back to Manaus to resupply after our visit."

Wesley called out, "Mary! Get in here."

When an attractive young woman with brown skin and long, black hair joined us, Wesley looked at me and said, "Mary isn't her original name, obviously. But the first step in removing the savage from savages is to give them good Christian names." He turned his gaze toward Mary and added, "Tell Joshua and Ruth to move in with you for a few days. These people need to use their hut."

"Yes, father! God bless you, father!" She nodded and hurried out the door.

Tara bowed her head and said, "Thank you, Reverend Wilson. I can see already that you've done a fine job of turning these savages into good, well-mannered Christians!"

He puffed out his chest ever so slightly. "With God's help, Miss Kramer. With God's help."

She smiled shyly. "Please call me Tara."

As our conversation continued, Wesley warmed up to us. How much of that was genuine, I can't say. For our part, Tara and I did our best to come across as a fundamentalist Christian doctor and nurse who were naïve about life in the rainforest but trusting that God would guide us.

When Mary returned to lead us to our hut, Wesley invited us to dinner and went back to reading his Bible.

Our hut was at the far end of the village. Like all the huts, it featured rough vertical boards for walls and a thatch roof. Inside was little more than three hammocks strung from the ceiling, a table, some woven baskets, a collection of clay pots, and a few personal items. As Mary gave us a quick tour, she informed us that the village did all their cooking outdoors, and a community latrine was centrally located behind the huts.

As soon as Mary walked out the door, Tara exclaimed in a hushed voice, *"The Church of the Sacred Bleeding Heart of Jesus!* Are you crazy?"

"Hey, I was winging it. That was the first church name that came to mind. Besides, it's 1958. The Rolling Stones won't release 'Far Away Eyes' for another twenty years. How 'bout your acting job? That shy little come-on."

"One of us is gonna have to jam a trap-capsule in an orifice before Wesley knows what's happening. It may take a woman's touch to do it."

I looked up. "What do you think, Rodney?"

He materialized and said, "I think neither of you should do anything that might upset Wesley until we are closer to day three.

Remember, unless you steal a canoe, and paddle to who-knows-where, you have no other place to go."

"That seems like wise advice," I said. "We'll use today to get the lay of the land and have dinner with Wesley tonight. Tomorrow we will try to give everyone here physicals. I don't suppose you can time travel a doctor's bag to me, can you?"

"Sorry," Rodney said. "That is forbidden."

"Then I'll have to make one. Pharmaceutical scientists have derived many modern medicines from rainforest plants. Unfortunately, that wasn't a field I studied in college." I turned to Tara and asked, "How about you?"

She shook her head. "I wish I had."

"Rodney, will you be breaking any rules by being my medical encyclopedia and identifier of plants?"

"No. That is allowed."

"Good. Then that's what we'll do first. We'll take a hike through the rainforest, and you can look through Tara's and my eyes for medically useful plants. We will need plants for pain, infection, parasites, sexually transmitted diseases, and anything else that comes to mind."

Tara grabbed a couple of baskets that were sitting near the door. "We can put what we find in here."

Rodney popped out and back. "I checked with my supervisor and consulted my research tools. Did you know that Earth-humans have discovered only a small fraction of the useful plants in the Amazon Rainforest?"

"Sure," I said. "That's only logical."

"Unfortunately, deforestation is yet another way your species is dooming your survival. Who knows how many plants Earth-humans have already sent to extinction? Perhaps even species that could eliminate the next pandemic. The good news is that I now have knowledge of Earth's rainforest plants and their medical applications that are many years ahead of the most advanced scientific studies. Additionally, my supervisor has agreed to allow you to put into practice anything you remember about our finds when you return to present time."

I put a hand on Tara's shoulder. "This could be huge. We need to work together to remember everything we can."

"My mind shall be like that of a dog's mind in a forest full of squirrels."

"Huh?" I shot her a confused look.

"Haven't you watched the route Clarice takes in the woods near your cabin? She remembers every tree she's ever chased a squirrel up."

I smiled. "Let's go and inform Wesley of our plans, so he doesn't get suspicious. Minus the part about our receiving alien help, of course. It will actually make our doctor and nurse cover story more believable."

* * *

Upon hearing about our doctor's bag project, Wesley assigned two native men to us as rainforest guides. Even though he likely instructed them to lead us away from certain areas, the men turned out to be just what we needed.

Since neither Tara nor I had visited the Amazon Rainforest before, the mysteriousness of it was intimidating at first. But once we hiked for an hour or so without even one giant anaconda or massive jaguar attacking us, we began to relax and enjoy our surroundings. The heat, humidity, and smells made us feel as if we were in a giant greenhouse without the pots, and the sounds— from monkeys howling to frogs croaking to parrots squawking— were a constant reminder that wildlife was all around us.

With the help of the native men, we learned about the local terrain, hiked to the most promising locations for medically useful plants, and benefited from two extra sets of eyes. Despite

Tara's and my advantage of alien assistance, our guides turned out to be even more efficient at finding medicinal plants than we were —bringing us species that their people already knew about. With only a few exceptions, Rodney approved of their selections.

As we walked back toward the village, I picked up an apple-sized nut that some animal had hollowed out. I slipped it into my pocket, with thoughts of turning it into a primitive stethoscope.

We returned to our hut, drenched in sweat, ready to open our makeshift clinic.

* * *

That night we dined with Wesley outside in the center commons area, at an elaborately carved wooden table, lit by torches. There we got our first taste of the methods Wesley used to manipulate and abuse the native people. While he treated Tara and me as honored guests, all those who were not white had some sort of religious performance to complete before he would allow them to eat at a separate, less elaborate table. The youngest children had to sing; the middle children had to recite prayers; and the oldest children and the adults had to recite Bible verses. All of them seemed to be nervous about this, because if they failed in their task, a white assistant would lead them away without any food.

Wesley had seven white assistants to help him keep order. Four were men and three were women. The men were all young enough and big enough to command respect. The women were older and likely served as religious instructors.

Among the adult native people I observed, the men were in charge of hunting and fishing, and the women were in charge of food preparation, fabric and basket weaving, and whatever else Wesley required of them.

As the evening progressed, I watched closely for any hint that Ralph was occupying Wesley. While I saw none, Wesley's wary nature told me that inserting a trap-capsule in him would require a cunning maneuver on our part. Working in our favor was that the reverend was doing a poor job of concealing his glances at Tara. She noticed it too and flirted with him in response.

I waited until Wesley's attention was elsewhere before whispering to Tara, "I almost introduced you to Wesley as my wife. Now I'm glad I introduced you as my nurse instead. He obviously has a thing for you."

"Does that mean I get to be the superhero again?" she whispered back.

"It looks that way. Perhaps you can hide a trap-capsule in your mouth and give him a big, deep kiss."

She scowled. "Have you seen his teeth? I don't think he's brushed them in years. No way am I putting my tongue in that mouth!"

"Just continue flirting and keep a trap-capsule handy. When the opportunity arises, I'm sure you'll know where to stick it."

She scowled again—this time a bit more playfully.

A child screamed from a hut!

Tara and I lurched to our feet.

"Sit down!" Wesley ordered. "One of the children is receiving personalized Christian instruction—that's all."

"What do you mean by *personalized?*" I asked.

"Merely some corrections to encourage the child to perform better. All of them biblically authorized, of course."

Before we could sit, the child screamed again.

I took a quick step toward the hut and froze.

Tara did the same.

Rodney popped into our heads, waving his arms. "Whoa! Whoa! Do you know how difficult it is for me to stop both of you at the same time? Remember. You cannot go all superhero yet. If Ralph is here, and he figures out what you are up to, he will disappear faster than you can say *foreskin.* Do not take any action until you are closer to when your time travel window opens up. Then you can insert a trap-capsule into Wesley and use all your powers to light up this place if you want to. I am going to release you now. Please, calmly take your seats."

We did as he said.

"Foreskin?" Tara asked under her breath.

Rodney shrugged. "Sorry, I have been rereading the Bible to better understand why so many people use it to justify inhumanity. I was just at the section in Exodus where Zipporah took a flint knife and cut off her son's foreskin so she could touch Moses's feet with it. Go back to your flirting, Tara, but be aware that whether you are dealing with Wesley alone or Wesley occupied by Ralph, both are likely fighting feelings of guilt. Treat them like the bad boys they are."

We stayed on our best behavior for the rest of the evening, with me settling into the role of an easy-going Christian doctor, and Tara playing the conservative Christian nurse who, on Wesley's say-so, would toss aside her sexual repressions and let the reverend get biblical with her. All that acting belied the fact that whenever we heard another child cry out, every refurbished bone in our bodies begged to be set loose on a mission of mass destruction.

Chapter 20

The Rainforest Clinic

When morning arrived, we set up our makeshift clinic under a thatch canopy in the commons area. As we began seeing patients, Wesley watched over our operation and quite obviously made sure we saw only the healthiest people in the tribe. Since Tara and I intended to see everyone, and had two days to do so, we didn't object to the order of the patients. Getting an accurate count of the people under Wesley's influence was difficult, however. Men, women, and children were coming and going, and some, apparently, lived elsewhere along the river. In all, we saw over thirty children and fifteen adults on that first day. Seeing so many people prevented us from spending much time with anyone, so in that way, Wesley's reverse triage worked in our favor. Other than one patient with a broken finger, those who needed our attention suffered from either external parasites or infected cuts, which were treatable with the plants we had collected.

That evening was similar to the night before, with more biblical performances from members of the tribe, more denial of food for those who made mistakes, and more screaming from the huts. The only difference was that Tara and I were better prepared for the roles we were playing, which, in turn, helped us to gain Wesley's confidence.

Wesley's interest in Tara grew more fevered, too. But rather than taking that interest directly to her, he pulled me aside between dinner and dessert—almost as if we were high school buddies—first asking if Tara and I were involved with each other, then asking if she was involved with anyone, and finally asking if I thought Tara was interested in him. I assured him that Tara was uninvolved, likely a virgin, and had been troubled in the past by her sinful attraction to older clergy. As for whether she found him attractive, I said, "That's not something a doctor discusses with his nurse. But I've seen the way she looks at you."

Since seeing so many patients had exhausted Tara and me, we had a legitimate excuse to head to our hut soon after our meal. The main reason for our early departure, however, was to prevent Wesley from making an advance on Tara. Delaying the inevitable for another day served the dual purpose of building up his anticipation and moving us closer to when we could time travel the hell out of there.

* * *

When I awoke in the morning, the first thing I did was ask, "Rodney, what's our countdown?"

He materialized and replied, "Time travel becomes available in twenty-seven hours, thirteen minutes."

Tara and I washed up in the river, ate some of the fruit our patients had given to us, and opened our clinic. After the first few healthy patients, the next ones in line looked familiar. I whispered to Tara, "Haven't we seen these people before?"

"Yes. Wesley's sending them through again. Apparently, he thinks we can't tell one brown-skinned person from another."

"I'll be back." I set down the nut I had modified for a stethoscope, walked the short distance to Wesley's hut, and knocked on the open doorframe.

Wesley looked up from his hammock. "Doctor Westin. Come in! Come in! What's on your mind?"

"Why am I seeing the same patients I saw yesterday?"

He slid out of his hammock and stood. "Doctors—at least real ones—don't come around here too often. I guess you've become a celebrity."

"When I arrived two days ago, I saw children I haven't seen since then. I also haven't seen any of the children or young adults who were taken away from the table during meals."

He took a deep breath. "Those who do not devote themselves to properly studying the word of God must not benefit from God's gifts. Sometimes, the only way to remove the savage from a savage is through punishment and the withholding of rewards."

I too took a deep breath, only mine was to convince myself to refrain from seeing how far I could throw the reverend. "Listen. I'm a doctor, not a judge. A boat is supposed to pick up Tara and me sometime tomorrow. What you do here after we depart is your business, but I'm not leaving until I complete my mission, which is to see every so-called *savage* in this village."

He stared me down.

I met his stare with one of my own.

"Give me a half-hour," he finally said. "You'll get your patients."

I returned to the clinic and informed Tara that Wesley had relented.

Soon, one at a time, a dozen or so children and half as many adults emerged from the forest behind the huts. All could walk on their own, but many walked with obvious pain, and others squinted as if seeing the sun for the first time in a long time. For those patients, we moved the clinic inside our hut to give them the dignity of privacy.

The reason some people had difficulty walking became apparent with the first patient we saw: a boy, no older than ten, who had been sexually abused with a switch. And the boys weren't the only ones with genital injuries. The girls had them too.

The horrors Tara and I witnessed that day will likely give us a lifetime of nightmares. She sobbed between patients, and my throat burned as I held back doing the same.

Even Rodney was affected. After we finished treating the last patient, he materialized, wearing all black, and said solemnly, "I am sorry for exposing both of you to this. Learning about such things via my research is nothing compared to seeing it through your eyes. If Ralph is here, catch him, and I will see that he is punished. If Wesley is acting on his own, I will leave the punishment up to you and hope it is severe."

"Oh, he's going down tonight," Tara spat. She scanned the hut for scattered medical supplies and began consolidating them on a table. "Either way," she added under her breath.

"Keep in mind," said Rodney, "that Wesley could not do what he has done without help. Just as in politics, where some people vote against themselves, the same applies here. Many in the tribe are fierce supporters of both Wesley and his methods. They believe he gets his orders directly from God."

I nodded and said, "That seems to be a common theme throughout Earth's history—from the Spanish Inquisition to Donald Trump—authoritarian leaders who create a version of God that shares their hate and prejudices and then use that god as a vehicle to convince others to commit atrocities they would not otherwise commit."

"Actually, it started much earlier than the Spanish Inquisition," Tara added.

Rodney hung his head in silence.

I looked up and said, "I guess that's why the three of us are here. Isn't it, Rodney? Your people tried to help, became unwitting gods, and it backfired."

He smiled sadly. "Unfortunately, my people are not all-knowing. All we can do now is try to make things right."

Mary knocked on the doorframe. "Dinner is ready."

"We'll be right there." I waited for Mary to walk out of earshot before saying to Tara, "It's superhero time. After dinner, I'll leave early, so you can be alone with Wesley. Make sure you have a trap-capsule handy—and good luck."

"She will not be totally alone," Rodney corrected. "I will be there too and will alert you if Tara is in danger."

"For once, Rodney, I'll be glad to have you watching my every move," Tara said.

Chapter 21

Bad Boys Get Spanked

D inner proceeded as it had the previous two nights, with tribal members—young and old—singing and reciting in exchange for the reward or punishment that followed. The difference on this night was that Tara sat as close to Wesley as she could, while turning on the charm.

Although I knew she was just acting, watching the woman I love come on to another man wasn't easy—a touch of an arm, a smile, a laugh, a blush—all of it subtle, yet so convincing.

When I excused myself to go to bed early, Tara looked at me and announced loudly, "Oh, it's our last night here, and I'm not that tired. I'm gonna stay up a bit longer. I'm so fascinated by all the good work Reverend Wilson is doing here." She turned to Wesley and continued, "Perhaps he can teach me more about his methods for turning savages into Christians!"

Yeah, her last line would have alerted most thinking men that they were being played. But at that moment, Wesley wasn't thinking with his brain.

I settled into our hut and tried to use my enhanced hearing to follow what Tara and Wesley were saying to each other. I could hear their voices just fine. The problem with my hearing was that I hadn't yet mastered how to make it directional—if that were even possible. Therefore, the more I concentrated on their conversation, the more distracting competing conversations became, as well as the many animal calls in the rainforest.

I summoned my planetary consultant, second class. "Rodney, I need you."

He materialized, still wearing black. "Yes, Stefan."

"I thought my enhanced hearing would make it easy for me to listen to Tara and Wesley, but it's only increasing the noise. Can you give me a play-by-play?"

"Sure. Do you want simulated or neutral voices? Full or partial details?"

"Simulated voices, I guess. But limit the details to what I might read in a book. I don't need to know every single expression or step they take."

Tara's voice came out of Rodney's mouth: "How does a man like you take care of his needs in a place like this?"

Wesley's voice came out of Rodney's mouth: "It's difficult. But the Lord provides."

Rodney's voice (well, actually Trevor Noah's voice) came out of Rodney's mouth: "They are looking into each other's eyes. I do not know if this is too much detail, but Wesley's expression is what I would call *lecherous*."

The weirdness of having a one-man radio show playing in my head was almost as distracting as the competing sounds my hearing had picked up.

Tara's voice: "Do you think, perhaps, the Lord has sent me?"

Wesley's voice: "Oh, most definitely."

Rodney's voice: "Tara has let her hand fall upon Wesley's hand."

Tara's voice: "I think Doctor Westin feels a little uneasy about your punishment methods. But not me."

Rodney's voice: "She has turned her head. I think she is trying to look shy. Now she is turning back."

Tara's voice: "I don't know how or why, but the punishments have awakened something in me."

Rodney's voice: "Wesley's expression has changed to one of amusement."

Wesley's voice: "What awakens you more—the thought of giving a punishment or the thought of receiving a punishment?"

Tara's voice: "Both, actually. I guess . . . since these feelings are all so new for me, giving would be a better way to start."

Rodney's voice: "Wesley is trembling."

Tara's voice: "I guess I should have mentioned my feelings to you before dinner, while there were still savages in need of punishment. Oh, well. It's too late now. I should probably head back to my hut anyway."

Wesley's voice: "Don't go. You must hear my confession. I have had lustful feelings for you since the day you arrived. The Lord, who sees all, is angry with me for that sin. He will destroy everything I've built here, unless you see to it that I am properly punished."

My voice: "Bingo!"

Rodney's voice: "They are standing up. Wesley is leading Tara to his hut. They are going inside."

Rodney's image froze.

Silence.

More silence.

My voice: "Rodney, are you there? What's happening?"

Rodney's voice (his image moving again): "Sorry. I got caught up in watching."

My voice: "Watching what?"

Rodney's voice: "One moment."

Silence.

My voice (desperate): *"Rodney!"*

Rodney's voice: "Tara is sitting sideways in a hammock—partially undressed. She has some sort of whip—perhaps a riding crop—in her right hand. Wesley has removed all his clothes and is standing at attention."

Tara's voice (sultry): "Have you been a bad boy?"

Wesley's voice (childlike): "Yes, ma'am."

Tara's voice: "Do you know what happens to bad boys?"

Wesley's voice: "No, ma'am."

Tara's voice (like a dominatrix): "Bad boys get spanked!"

My voice: "She set that all up, just so she could quote Chrissie Hynde of the Pretenders!"

Rodney's voice: "She is patting her lap."

Tara's voice (like a dominatrix): "Come here. Get spanked!"

My voice: "Yep. Chrissie Hynde."

Rodney's voice: "Oh, that had to hurt. Do you want me to repeat Wesley's cries for you?"

My voice: "That's okay. I can hear them from here."

Rodney's voice: "She has whipped him six or seven times. Ooh! The welts. Hold on. I am switching to conference mode. Tara, stop! Insert the trap-capsule. *Now!*"

Tara's voice: "You've been a bad, bad boy!"

Rodney's voice: "She is still whipping him—even harder. Now, Tara!"

Tara's voice (irritated): "Fine!"

Wesley's voice: "Sweet Mother of Jesus! No woman has ever done that to me before. What did you stick up my—"

Rodney's voice (interrupting): "Ralph is not here! It was all Wesley."

Tara's voice (even more irritated): *"What!"*

Rodney's voice: "You can quit now. The trap-capsule insertion was successful. Unfortunately, I picked the wrong missionary. I am sorry."

Tara's voice: "Do you know what, Wesley? This isn't the turn-on I thought it would be."

Wesley's voice (pleading): "But we're just getting started."

Tara's voice: "Perhaps *you* are. I'm finished."

Rodney's voice: "Tara has pushed Wesley onto the floor. She is standing and putting on her clothes—being careful not to use her right index finger. Now Wesley is standing too—albeit gingerly. He has grabbed Tara's shoulder to prevent her from leaving. And there he goes—flying through the air, through the wall, and landing outside on the dirt! Tara has paused to admire her work and—"

Tara's voice (interrupting): "I'll take it from here, Rodney. Tara is walking out the door, with her index finger held in the air. Soon she'll reach her lover's hut, where he will be waiting with the strongest disinfectant the rainforest can provide."

* * *

We used our enhanced hearing that evening to listen for signs that Wesley was organizing a posse to take revenge. Even though we could outrun everyone in the village, a night of hiding in the rainforest was a frightening prospect—especially since we couldn't run faster than a venomous snake could strike. Fortunately, Wesley had no reason to hurry. After all, as far as he knew, all he had to do was divert the boat that was supposed to pick us up, and we'd be trapped.

Once we grew confident that nothing would happen that night, we discussed with Rodney what we were going to do—both in the morning and in the coming days. After all, Tara and I couldn't just time travel back home when the window opened up and purge the abused children from our thoughts. As a remedy for that, Rodney offered to attempt a limited memory wipe.

We passed.

Chapter 22

Just Like Jackie Chan

At sunrise, I opened my eyes and asked, "Rodney, what's our countdown?"

He materialized and replied, "Time travel becomes available in three hours, forty-seven minutes."

I lay in my hammock for a bit before sitting up and listening. Footsteps were approaching.

I dropped to the floor and shook Tara. "Wake up."

She rolled out of her hammock, and we both hurried to the door to look outside.

Four men were almost to our hut—two white men with knives and two native men with blowguns.

"Weapons?" Tara asked. "Rodney, you said nothing about weapons."

"Both of you are quick enough to disarm the men with the knives," he said. "But those blowguns are almost certainly armed with darts dipped in poison from poison dart frogs."

"Is the poison powerful enough to kill a human?" I asked.

"It depends on the frog," he said. "If they have access to the most poisonous ones, the answer is absolutely yes."

I stepped through the doorway. "Hello, gentlemen. What brings you here on this fine morning?"

"Your trial for the perverted seduction of an apostle of God is to begin immediately," said the taller of the white men.

"My trial? I haven't seduced an apostle of God since I arrived in Brazil."

"He means the woman," said the shorter white man.

I looked back over my shoulder. "Tara, it's for you!"

* * *

The men escorted us to the center of the village, where Wesley was waiting in a tall, padded, wide-armed throne that had been carved from a tree trunk. He was dressed in full preacher regalia, with two additional knife-carrying white men standing to each side, and a large wooden altar separating him from Tara and me.

Tara glowered at Wesley before saying, "My, that's quite a pillow you're sitting on." She scanned the audience of tribal members who had gathered around. Some were standing, but most were sitting on the ground. She turned back to face Wesley. "Why do you get to be all comfy, while these people don't even get simple chairs to sit on? I guess you're just one big pain in the ass!"

Wesley pounded on the arm of his chair with a gavel made from a coconut and shouted, "Silence!" He pointed to the altar and said to the men by his side, "Tie her down."

"Do not resist," said Rodney, who had returned to verbal mode. "All you have to do is delay for a little over three hours, and I will get you out of here."

"I may not have that much time," Tara whispered, as she allowed the men to escort her to the altar, where they pushed her onto her back and secured her with ropes made from vines.

Once Wesley was satisfied that Tara had been properly restrained, he announced, "The Lord Jesus Christ speaks through me. He has found Miss Tara Kramer guilty of the perverted seduction of an apostle of God and hereby sentences her to thirty-nine tocandera stings."

A native man carried a small wooden box over to the altar, placed a pair of wooden tweezers on top of it, and set them both at Tara's feet.

I whispered, "Rodney, what's a tocandera?"

"One moment. . . . It is another name for a bullet ant."

"I was afraid of that. Can the stings kill her?"

"Studies suggest that bullet ants are the insect with the world's most painful sting. She can survive numerous stings. Whether she can survive thirty-nine depends on her reaction to the venom."

I was still standing in front of Wesley, when I looked at him with all the contempt I could muster and said, "Your men told us there would be a trial. Before you administer any punishment, I demand that trial!"

He glared down at me from his throne. "The Lord Jesus Christ knows all. He has already held Miss Kramer's trial up in heaven and found her guilty."

I clutched each side of my head and screamed, "Wait! Wait! Incoming . . . The Lord Jesus Christ is now speaking through me. He has proclaimed Miss Kramer innocent and found that you, Reverend Wesley Wilson, have lied and are guilty of the perverted seduction of a virgin woman of God. He hereby sentences you to thirty-nine tocandera stings for the crime and six additional stings for the lie." I turned to the men standing beside Tara and pointed. "Release that innocent woman!"

Wesley pounded his gavel and shouted, "Silence, heretic! The Lord Jesus Christ speaks *only* through me."

"Really? Prove it."

Wesley's face contorted. "It's true because the Lord Jesus Christ has said so."

"Oh, yeah?" I challenged. "The Lord Jesus Christ has just told me that the only one who speaks through you is Satan!"

He pounded his gavel again. "Seize him!"

Two of the white men grabbed me—one on each arm—and the two native men raised their blowguns.

Wesley pushed himself out of his throne and approached the altar. He slid open a panel at the top of the wooden box, carefully grasped one of the bullet ants with the tweezers, and slid the panel closed. He looped around the altar and waved the ant under my nose. "The Lord Jesus Christ has just sentenced you to as many stings as this tocandera can deliver."

"Wait!" I shouted. "I have a confession to give. Surely I'm allowed to confess before receiving my punishment."

"Very well," he said. "Make it quick."

I closed my eyes and prayed, "Oh, dearest Lord . . . *Rodney*. I would like to confess my sinful desire to kick these men's asses. I know I have the strength to do so, but I'm a doctor, not a fighter. Please, oh Holy One, *Rodney*, guide me in what I'm about to do."

"Huh?" Rodney asked. "I do not know what you mean."

"Jesus Christ! Just take over my body, like you did when you typed that message on the Holy Laptop."

"I do not know how to fight either."

I took a deep, frustrated breath. "I ask that your divine eyes shine upon any movie starring Saint Bruce Lee or the Apostle Jackie Chan."

"Hold on."

I opened my eyes and said to Wesley, "The Lord is a little busy today. He put me on hold. He'll be right back."

He shook the bullet ant in my face again. "You have twenty seconds."

"Got it!" said Rodney. "Just give the word."

"Thank you, oh Lord, for hearing my confession. Now, please grant me one final request: deliver unto the men with the blowguns before they deliver unto me. I put myself into your hands. Let's kick some ass!"

I relaxed my body so Rodney could take over.

Nothing happened.

"Rodney!" I yelled.

Wesley pushed the bullet ant against my cheek!

I screamed as the sting lit up my face.

"Oh, I apologize," Rodney said. "I should have been clearer with my instructions. I thought that rather than being a puppet, you would enjoy some free will. Just imagine what you would like to do, and I will give you the coordination of either Jackie Chan or Bruce Lee."

I imagined slipping the men's hands, spinning, and delivering a kick to Wesley's forehead. Nothing happened.

Wesley applied the bullet ant to my other cheek.

"Fuuuck!" I screamed, as the pain pierced me. "Rodney!"

"I am still waiting for your choice: Jackie Chan or Bruce Lee?"

"Jackie Chan!"

"Okay. The coordination is his, but the speed and power are yours. Now put some muscle into it!"

Wesley never saw what hit him! Neither did the men on my arms. The men with the blowguns were more troubling. I dove out of the way of the first man's shot, ducked behind Wesley's throne, reached around for his gavel, pitched a strike into the chest of the second man, and then tackled and knocked the wind out of the first man before he could reload. After snapping the blowguns into pieces, all I had to worry about were the two additional white men, but they fled into the rainforest when I turned in their direction. The entire fight was over within seconds.

Up to that moment, I had successfully avoided getting into a fight for my entire life (except for that girl who beat me up when I was in the third grade). Now that I had finally been in one, I wasn't sure how to feel about it. Being able to move like a martial arts master, while using the strength and quickness of my refurbished limbs, was exhilarating. On the other hand, I had been trained to help people, not hurt them. That all the men gave up quickly, and I didn't have to injure anyone seriously, was a relief.

As the tribe watched on, I reached down and pulled Wesley to his feet.

"Hey, what about me?" Tara asked.

I looked over at her, still tied to the altar. "Break your own ropes."

Her middle finger found freedom.

I wasn't trying to be an asshole. Really. Instead, I was hoping Tara would have the strength to break free, thereby leaving a lasting impression on our observers.

She struggled for a bit before snapping the ropes.

Her display of strength, along with my victory in combat, produced the desired result. We were now the tribe's de facto leaders. After informing the tribe that we didn't represent any god, and would be leaving soon, we took advantage of our leadership position just long enough to advise them to return to their traditional ways and, if possible, avoid contact with missionaries in the future.

Our final task was to supervise the pack-up and departure of Reverend Wesley Wilson and all his people. I suppose I could have used my strength and fighting ability to further beat into them that what they did here would never be tolerated again, but violence just isn't my thing. That they would have to survive a long, unplanned canoe trip back to Manaus was punishment enough.

As Tara and I escorted Wesley and his contingent to the riverbank, everyone in the tribe turned their backs to them. The two of us, however, weren't as unsociable. We even helped the missionaries load up their canoes with supplies, including a very special wooden box surreptitiously placed under Wesley's seat, with its top panel slid open—just a little.

Tara and I waved as the missionaries departed and watched them disappear downriver. We stayed on the riverbank, using our enhanced hearing, until we heard the inevitable screams.

Every animal species on Earth has an important role to play. The bullet ants had just played theirs.

I looked up and asked, "Rodney, what's our countdown?"

"The countdown ended almost two hours ago. You can depart whenever you wish."

Leaving the tribe was more complicated than we expected. We tried saying goodbye and departing via the path we had arrived on, but the children grabbed our hands and insisted on accompanying us. Disappearing while in their view, or anyone else's view, risked starting a whole other religion. Our ultimate solution was to borrow a dugout canoe, which we used to float downstream until we were out of sight.

"Rodney!" Tara called out. "Take us home."

Chapter 23

A Short Chapter

U pon reaching the cabin, the first thing I did was write down everything I could remember about rainforest plants and their medical uses. Then I looked at my face in the bathroom mirror. Large red welts adorned each cheek. "Rodney," I summoned, "we're gonna have to delay our next time travel mission."

He materialized and sauntered to the front of my brain, where he leaned sideways into my sight to view my reflection in the mirror. "Oh, my! Would you like some refurbished cheeks? I can order some up for you. Perhaps with dimples?"

"No!"

He turned to face the inside of my head. "Then I suppose a delay is appropriate."

"That would be nice. How about a week?"

"How about two days?"

"How about three?"

"That is acceptable. I will turn off my visual image and stay out of your way until then. If you change your mind and wish to leave sooner, just give me a shout-out."

* * *

My bullet ant stings gradually mellowed to resemble wasp stings. By the time day three arrived, Tara was able to apply some of her makeup to my welts, making me presentable for wherever we were going.

Rodney materialized the moment she finished with my face. "Knock! Knock! Good morning, humans. Shall we plan your next jump?"

"Let us at least get out of the bathroom first," I said.

Tara and I moved to the kitchen, where she poured us each a coffee, and I gave Clarice fresh bowls of food and water.

We took our seats and Tara asked, "Where are we traveling to today?"

"Since we have confirmed that Ralph was not occupying Wesley Wilson, we now have access to any date earlier than your April 21, 2013 meeting with Fred Phelps. The challenge we have is that the list of people who do evil in the name of Christianity is practically endless. Even if we limited our search to pedophile priests and ministers, you would die of old age before we could investigate even a fraction of them."

"What about someone like Jerry Falwell Jr. or Joel Osteen?" I asked. "I doubt they abuse children, but they certainly abuse scripture and use Christianity as a profit center. If I correctly understand your explanation of Ralph's mindset, they would be prime candidates. After all, if the pain of dying by crucifixion made Ralph hate the human race and go rogue, who better for him to occupy than someone who makes insane profits from those who wear crosses around their necks?"

A thoughtful expression graced Rodney's face. "Although I cannot say with certainty that Ralph has never occupied Falwell or Osteen, I believe the odds are against it."

"Why?" I asked.

"Remember what I said about Ralph sticking with one primary person throughout the most malevolent years of that person's life and only dabbling in side projects when he gets bored?"

"Sure," I said.

"That applies here. In the original timeline, Donald Trump was Ralph's main contemporary subject, and any side project human he amused himself with would have been uncomplicated, like Fred Phelps. Since people such as Falwell and Osteen are worth tens of millions of dollars and run complicated business operations, we can reason that neither was a side project during the timeline of Trump. Accordingly, if we eliminate Falwell and Osteen as being occupied by Ralph in the original timeline, we must also do the same in this new timeline, because my research detects no difference in their behavior."

Tara laughed. "I guess for some people, abhorrent behavior just comes naturally."

"You sent Tara dreams about a Catholic priest who was molesting a young boy, and a minister who was whipping a native child at school in Canada. You also sent me dreams about slavery in the South, the Salem witch trials, and the Spanish Inquisition. Are those all on our definite time travel list?"

"Yes. Except if we catch Ralph before we finish the list. So unless one of you has a recommendation for a person I have not thought of, I suggest we stick to that list. Chronologically, next in line are multiple abusive Christian residential schools in Canada and a particularly egregious Catholic school run by priests in Italy. The time-periods are similar, allowing you to time travel to one location a little earlier than the other. Since I am not doing a good job of being decisive, I will let you two decide. Where would you like to go first?"

"Italy!" we exclaimed in unison.

Chapter 24

Silent Revenge

I taly in the 1950s was in the midst of recovery under the Marshall Plan, but in Verona, at the Saint Zoticus Catholic School for the Deaf, students were experiencing horrors from which they would never recover. On the boys' side of the school, more than a half-dozen priests aroused themselves by anally raping students. And on the opposite side of the church, where the girls were, a similar number of priests fulfilled their desires by forcing students to give them hand jobs during confession. No matter which side of the school the students attended, those who resisted the priests were beaten, required to kneel in corners for hours, or punished in other ways.

One problem for this mission was that Rodney didn't have a specific person for us to investigate. If Ralph was there, he could be occupying any of the priests or even a nun. Another problem was figuring out how to speak with the students. Italian Sign Language was well developed at the time, but neither Tara nor I knew anything about it. Rodney, who already spoke over ninety languages, had to be a quick study and add both Italian and Italian Sign Language to his repertoire. To communicate, we'd relax our arms and speak in English. Rodney would then make the appropriate Italian words come out of our mouths while signing at the same time. Although sometimes Rodney came across as a little naïve and childlike, that he could simultaneously translate two languages and do it quickly enough for two people, made me wonder how much of his behavior was an act. In this instance, he truly was a superior species.

Per our request, Rodney looked up Italy's weather records and chose a beautiful spring week in 1957. Tara had to depart dressed as a nun, and I had to go as a priest. Even though our uniforms made us both feel awkward, they provided plenty of pocket space for money and other necessities. Once we arrived, we checked into a hotel and did a little shopping for everyday clothing. We also argued with Rodney that it was both ridiculous and dangerous to attempt to infiltrate the school before we completed our required three-day stay.

We won that argument, rented a car, and enjoyed a marvelous four-day Italian vacation before Rodney threatened to leave us forever in 1957, if we didn't get to work.

On the morning of the fifth day, we entered the boys' side of the school—a brown two-story stucco building—using a cover story that Archbishop Giovanni Urbani had sent us to observe the entire school. That cover story was effective for all of forty-five minutes before six priests, armed with scepters, confronted us in a hallway. Apparently, this is why people experienced in undercover operations undergo months of preparation and training instead of just time traveling in and winging it.

A stout priest, who appeared to be the oldest of the bunch, scowled at us and said, "I called the archbishop's office. No one sent any observers. Who are you and—"

The rest of the man's words were in untranslated Italian.

I tried to respond, but everything I said remained in English.

Tara attempted to take over and experienced the same results.

"Rodney," I called out. "We've lost translation."

Silence.

"Rodney!" Tara shouted. "Are you there?"

An image of Clarice appeared in our heads. "I am sorry," the dog said in a woman's voice. "Rodney is unavailable. How may I help you?"

The priests grabbed our arms!

I ignored the men and said, "What do you mean, Rodney is unavailable?"

"He got called away. But do not worry. You are in good hands. I am a full-time planetary consultant, third class. And as you can see, I have picked an important person in both of your lives as my avatar. You can call me *Fluffy*. I am going to put you on a brief hold to review your case, and then we can get started." She vanished.

"Oh, great," Tara said sarcastically. "A dog has put us on hold."

Unsure of what to do, Tara and I let the men lead us through a long hallway and down the steps to the basement. There we entered a large, dimly lit room, with chains affixed to the walls and multiple tables containing leather restraints and corded sex toys that didn't look as if they were meant to give pleasure to the person on the receiving end.

We continued trying to speak to the priests and didn't offer any resistance. These priests weren't frail old men, nor were their scepters fragile ceremonial staffs. Instead, all the men appeared to be younger than fifty, and their scepters the equivalent of police batons.

If Rodney were providing us with Jackie Chan's fighting ability, I would've had no doubt we could defeat the men. Without such help, the chances were good that someone would be able to knock us unconscious with a scepter before we could take down even two or three of them. The thought of waking up chained to a wall was terrifying.

"Fluffy!" I shouted. "Where are you? We need language translation, now!"

She flashed in. "One moment, please." She flashed out.

Another priest entered the room and approached where we were standing. This one had a chiseled face and was more elaborately dressed than the others were. He began speaking.

When we shrugged to show we didn't understand, his voice grew angry.

Fluffy materialized. "I have reviewed your case and have good news. I will be able to make you speak and understand English."

"English? That's what we're speaking now!" I said.

"No, you are not. You are speaking Malay."

"Malay!" I pivoted toward Tara. "Can you read my lips?"

She shot me a surprised look. "No! I would've noticed sooner, but the whole dog-in-my-head-priests-on-my-arms thing has been a bit of a distraction."

"Yeah, I can relate."

"Oh! Now I see it," Fluffy said. "When Rodney departed, I switched both of you to the auto translator, but there appears to be a problem."

"No shit," I replied, before waving a finger in front of the well-dressed priest, hoping he would understand I needed more time.

The priest shut up long enough to summon a menacing stink eye.

"How 'bout just getting us out of here?" Tara asked.

"I am a temporary fill-in. Only the planetary consultant in charge of your case can do that."

"Can you at least give us Jackie Chan's fighting ability?" I asked.

"Let me check." She flashed out and back. "I do not see anything in the customer service notes about a Jackie Chan. I can research that some more, or you can wait until Rodney returns."

The well-dressed priest resumed his tirade.

"We don't have time," I said quickly. "Is there any way to fix the problem with the auto translator?"

"I can reboot and try a manual override. From what language to what language?" she asked.

I balled my fists. "English to Italian!"

"One moment please. . . . There. . . . That should do it. Shout out for me if you need anything else."

As Fluffy vanished, the well-dressed priest's words became intelligible. ". . . and if you don't tell me now, life will get very uncomfortable for you!"

"My apologies," I said. "This has all been a terrible mistake. We will be leaving now."

"You're not going anywhere until I get some answers," he replied.

"How about *you* giving *us* some answers?" Tara demanded. "Why does a school, run by a church, need . . ." She paused to sweep her hand toward the shackles on the near wall. "A torture chamber?"

"A torture chamber?" He laughed. "What makes you think this is a torture chamber? These are merely restraints. Some of our students are feebleminded, and we must temporarily restrain them so they do not hurt themselves."

Tara pointed to a long metal item on a nearby table. "And how does a rectal probe restrain a child?"

His face tightened. "I will *not* be questioned by a woman!"

"How about a man, then?" I asked in an irritated voice. "What kind of sick fuck gets his jollies from molesting children?"

I wasn't sure how the word *fuck* translated into Italian, or if the system Fluffy had us on was even capable of such a translation. The well-dressed priest answered my question by turning toward his associates and commanding, "Restrain them!"

I looked at Tara and gave her the slightest nod. Though we weren't trained fighters, we didn't know when Rodney would return. Risking a blow to the head from a scepter was a much better option than risking torture while chained to a wall.

Adding to the urgency of our situation was my feeling that Ralph was occupying the well-dressed priest. There was just something about his infrequently blinking eyes that reminded me of my encounter with Ralph in Massachusetts. I slid a hand into my pocket, grasped a trap-capsule, and charged! I was so fast that the well-dressed priest didn't have time to react. As I tackled him to the floor, I jammed the trap-capsule into his ear.

"Fluffy, now!" I shouted.

She reappeared. "Now, what?"

"The trap-capsule! Grab Ralph!"

"Hold please." She disappeared.

Three men seized me, while another pounded his scepter into my kidneys, my shoulder, and the back of my head. The final blow sent a flash of light through my vision and a shot of pain through my body. I didn't pass out, but for a moment my limbs lost all their strength. The men yanked me to my feet and slammed me backward onto a table.

I turned my head right and left, looking for Tara. My eyes focused on an unconscious priest—his knee bent at a most unnatural angle. A little beyond him was the final priest—one hand around Tara's chest and the other holding a syringe to her neck.

The well-dressed priest grabbed my chin and held the trap-capsule before my eyes. "Nice try. But this one appears to be a dud."

Fluffy reappeared. "Oh, *that* trap-capsule! Activating now." She paused for a moment. "Sorry. He was not there. Better luck next time." She disappeared.

I glared at the well-dressed priest. "How's it going, Ralph?"

"Ralph? I hate that name! Call me Jesus."

"No. I like Ralph," I said.

He waved a hand dismissively and said, "Whatever. When I'm

done with you and your female friend, you'll be lucky if you can say your own name." He made a fist around the trap-capsule and knocked on my forehead. "Hello! Who's in there?"

"Fluffy," I replied.

"Fluffy? I don't know a Fluffy."

"I think she's new—a planetary consultant, third class."

His face pinched up. "Third class!"

"Yes."

He shook his head. "I don't get any respect. . . . Full-time or part-time?"

"Full-time."

"Well, at least that's something." He reached to his side, pulled a tray table closer, set the trap-capsule on it, and smashed the capsule with a ball peen hammer. His eyes moved from one priest to another as he commanded, "Strap him down tight and suspend her from the wall."

The men who had slammed me to the table rearranged themselves. One collected the scepters and set them on a nearby table before walking over to assist the man who was holding the syringe against Tara's neck. Together, they escorted her backward to the wall and shackled her left wrist. At the same time, two of the men positioned themselves to better hold down my shoulders, while another secured my right wrist with a leather strap.

That was enough to satisfy Ralph that we were under control. He turned on his heels, said, "I'm going to my office to get my tools," and hurried up the stairs.

When will villains ever learn not to abandon the heroes of the story?

Using only half of my strength, I playfully resisted the men attempting to secure my left wrist.

I whispered softly, so only Tara could hear me, "Let them shackle you. I've got this."

When she went limp, I picked up my resistance.

The two men quickly secured Tara's other arm, allowing the

man with the syringe to kneel to secure her feet. The other man rushed over to help his associates restrain me.

I imagined what was going to happen and then did it. Using all my strength, I pulled my arms together, breaking the leather strap and catching two heads in the middle. They collided with a sickening crack! I wheeled off the table and caught the next man's hand as he reached for a scepter. A snap of my wrist dislocated his elbow.

I wasn't fast enough to prevent the last man—the biggest of the bunch—from grabbing a scepter. We locked eyes as he confidently tossed the weapon from one hand to the other.

Suddenly the syringe-man flew into the big man's back! They both crumpled to the floor.

I gave each a painful yet medically safe punch to make sure they didn't get up.

I looked over at Tara—two arms and one leg shackled to the wall—and said, "Nice kick."

"Hey, I couldn't let you have all the fun. Come get me down."

I stroked my chin. "Hmm. . . . I don't know. The sight of you all trussed up like that is strangely arousing."

She stuck her tongue out at me.

"Any idea where the key is?" I asked.

Ralph returned through the door, carrying a leather bag. He glanced at all the incapacitated priests and huffed. "Good help is so hard to come by these days."

I sat on the edge of a table, facing Ralph, and said, "We have another trap-capsule. Why don't you make things easy for all of us and let me send you home? Surely your planet is more to your liking than Earth."

He steepled his fingers and raised them to his chest. "I've had hundreds of years to think about that. As tempting as your offer is, I'm going to say no. Revenge is too addicting, and now that I know people are pursuing me, it adds to the fun. Is this the first time we've met?"

"No."

"Oh, good. That means I've already won at least one round."

"All Tara and I have to do is win once."

"I suppose we could fight it out right now, mano a mano."

"Let's do it."

He looked around the room. "Then again, you might get lucky with your second trap-capsule before I have a chance to vacate this body. Therefore, I think not."

"Coward!"

"Ooh, that hurts. I'll try to be braver the next time we meet. Salem, perhaps? Until then . . ." He raised a hand and waved with just his fingers. "Toodle-oo!"

The body Ralph had been occupying slumped slightly before its original occupant regained control and raced up the stairs.

I gave chase and caught the man halfway to the first floor. "I won't hurt you, if you tell me where to find the key for the shackles."

He answered in a shaky voice, "It's in the black desk, in the corner, second drawer."

I let the man go with a warning that if he left the building or called the police I would expose him as a child molester. Then I returned to the basement, where I found the key and got to work on Tara's shackles.

As I unlocked the last one, Tara said, "When Rodney returns, he has a hell of a lot of explaining to do."

Rodney materialized, wearing purple one-piece footie pajamas. "Did someone say my name?" He twisted around to secure the loose flap over his buttocks.

"Where have you been!" Tara demanded. "We had Ralph caught, but your replacement blew it, and we lost him."

"Oh, dear. I am so sorry."

"That's it?" I asked. "We risked our lives; had Ralph right where we wanted him; and all you can say is you're sorry?"

He pulled up his virtual chair and sat. "My species is very different from yours. Even though many of us are capable of leaving our bodies to occupy other beings, on our home planet, we prefer to remain in our physical bodies. I am sure you have screamed the phrase *holy shit* many times in your life."

"Of course," I said.

"We shouted our version of those words long before your people ever did. Think of how many months an average human wastes sitting on the toilet in a lifetime. My species was the same way until genetic engineering allowed us to reduce that toilet-time to a single event each year. Unfortunately, we cannot always predict when that event will happen. But when it arrives, it comes on suddenly and takes a long time to complete because . . . Well, you get the picture."

"Holy shit," I said.

"Holy shit," he echoed. "But I feel *much* better now!"

"Then I guess we're ready to go home," I said.

"No!" said Tara. "Ralph being gone won't stop the priests and nuns here from molesting the children. We must put a stop to that—even if it's only temporary."

"She's right. Give us both Jackie Chan's fighting ability, and be ready to pull us back to present time at a moment's notice. We need to destroy everything in this torture chamber and scare the living shit out of everyone who works here."

"Bruce Lee was a better fighter," Tara said. "I want his ability."

* * *

After ripping out the junction box where all the phone lines came in, Tara and I got to work using two distinct fighting styles and the strength that few, if any, humans on Earth could match. Our abilities turned out to be more useful for destroying devices in the basement than for kicking priestly ass, however. Without Ralph's leadership, only a few people resisted. That was disappointing, until we concluded that embarrassment would be a more effective deterrent than breaking bones anyway.

We gathered the priests, nuns, and support staffs from both sides of the school and blindfolded them in a large room, where we used Italian Sign Language to ask the children to point out their molesters. Those people we stripped naked, tied together at the wrist, and wrote in big black letters across their chests, "I molest children." Then we led the entire line of them out to the sidewalk in front of the church, secured them between two lamp-posts, and removed their blindfolds.

Even though they were already naked, we further dressed down the molesters with a threat that we would return with a worse punishment if any of them ever touched a child again.

We concluded our mission by stepping back inside and watching from an upstairs window until gawkers halted traffic and began taking pictures.

With great sadness and a little satisfaction, I called out, "Rodney, take us home."

Chapter 25

Shame on Canada, eh?

I was sitting at the kitchen table, doing research on my computer, when I looked up and said, "Rodney, I think we should skip Canada."

He materialized, wearing skates and a Team Canada hockey jersey, and asked, "Why?"

I did my best to maintain a straight face and said, "Because if it's true that Ralph sticks with one primary person throughout the most malevolent years of that person's life, I think that person was the priest we encountered in Verona. Therefore, if he was involved in the abuse and deaths of indigenous people at Christian residential schools in Canada, it was likely as a temporary side project. It's not that the abuse was any less in Canada. In fact, I think it was worse. But considering that you said the time frames were similar, do you think Ralph would rather hang out in a remote school in Canada, where it's cold in the winter and the mosquitos could carry him away in the summer, or in Italy, where the weather is milder and the territory oozes with history and culture?"

Rodney skated from one side of my head to the other before

executing an Olympics-worthy jump and spin. "Skating is not cultural?"

I cringed. "Certainly not when you're doing it in my brain! I know I'm only seeing an image, but just the thought of skate blades slicing around up there is giving me a headache."

His skates vanished, leaving him standing in socks. "The time frames do not have to be similar. Canada's residential school system operated from 1876 to 1996, and during much of that time, white authorities could forcibly separate indigenous children from their families. Those children were subjected to malnourishment and both physical and sexual abuse. At least six thousand of them died. The Canadian government administered and funded the schools, and the Roman Catholic, Anglican, Presbyterian, and United churches ran them."

I looked at Rodney as skeptically as I could look at someone who was inside my head. "Sure, we could go earlier. But the abuse in Canada's residential schools was so widespread that it would be almost impossible to find Ralph. Unless, of course, you have a specific person in mind."

"Hold on." He flashed out.

Tara, who was sitting opposite me at the kitchen table, looked up from the research she was doing on her smartphone. "If we can help in any way, we must do so. When I think of Canadians, the image that comes to mind is that they are the nicest people on Earth. While overall that may be true, what they did to those indigenous children was hideous. Canada's goal was to assimilate the children into a white European colonial culture. Separating them from their families was just the start. They took away their native beliefs and traditions and forced them to become Christians. As part of that cultural genocide, they cut the children's hair short, dressed them in European-style clothing, and forbade them from speaking their native language. Those who violated the rules were severely punished. Among the punishments the Christian leaders subjected the children to were tongue-piercings with needles, if they spoke their native language; locking them in cages, if they tried to escape; and shocking them, if they committed various other violations."

I shook my head in disgust. "I haven't attended church in years, but when I did, the minister frequently preached that Jesus wanted people to be loving and kind to each other. While I don't doubt that many Christians live up to that ideal, the dark side of the religion frequently outweighs the bright side. Seemingly every generation produces multiple influential Christian groups that thrive by hating and abusing others."

"Each of those generations also produces multiple Christian groups that generously contribute to society through charity work," Tara added.

"That's true. But do good deeds excuse bad deeds? We certainly wouldn't let serial killers, like Ted Bundy and Jeffrey Dahmer, off the hook because they volunteered at a soup kitchen or donated clothing to a homeless shelter, so why do we let Christianity—or any other religion with a long history of molestations and deaths—get a pass?"

Tara raised an eyebrow. "Probably because those with political power fear they will lose that power without the votes and campaign contributions those religions provide."

Rodney flashed back in. "I have reevaluated Canada and agree that what you two discovered in Italy eliminated any person I could propose for a 1950s Canadian visit. I do, however, have a strong candidate for another time. His name is Duncan Campbell Scott, and he was Canada's deputy superintendent of the Department of Indian Affairs from 1913 to 1932. What makes him a good Ralph-possibility is that in 1920 he succeeded in making Canada's dreadful assimilation program worse by making residential school attendance mandatory for every indigenous child between the ages of seven and sixteen."

"That will make three child abuse missions in a row," I said. "I've watched people slowly die in my hospital and felt less angst than I did in Brazil and Italy. I don't know how one gets beyond such feelings. Rodney, you saw the eyes of those children at the Saint Zoticus Catholic School for the Deaf. Even though we likely ended their torment, many of them were already dead inside, and they will remain that way until their physical death. I don't know if I can make it through something like that again."

Tara slid a chair next to me and put her head on my shoulder. "I've resigned myself to a lifetime of bad dreams. But this isn't about us. Any bad dreams we have are inconsequential compared to the real-life nightmares those children have experienced."

"You're right, Tara—of course. We'll do what we have to do."

"Do not fret," Rodney said. "Even though your Canadian mission will address child abuse, I doubt you will actually have to witness any children in pain."

"Why is that?" Tara asked.

"Because your target, Duncan Campbell Scott, seldom, if ever, actively participated in the abuse. Instead, he enabled and encouraged the churches to do it for him. Or, as he might have argued, 'do it for Canada.'"

I responded sarcastically, "Yeah, just what the churches needed —encouragement."

"What do you have in mind?" Tara asked.

"Remember when I said your refurbished livers could provide you with your most undervalued superpower? It is time to use those livers. Canada had a short wartime prohibition of alcohol that began in 1918. A visit with Duncan Campbell Scott in 1919 will likely find him eager for a drink. If you can convince him to consume more alcohol than he can handle, you should be able to insert a trap-capsule with little effort. If Ralph is there, we will do our best to catch him. If not, your accounts still have one sacrifice credit apiece, for your skin. Since Duncan's only child died before she could reproduce, you will have a timeline-safe option to use one of those credits to send Duncan to the depository planet before he makes residential schools mandatory for indigenous children."

"When do we leave?" I asked.

"Within the hour," he said.

* * *

We arrived in Ottawa, Ontario, early on a fall day, carefully selected to avoid the biting flies of summer and the first cold snap of winter. Since we wouldn't have the contacts necessary to acquire black market alcohol, Rodney provided us with two unmarked bottles of whiskey that we could fit into our oversized coat pockets. Our cover story for this time jump was that Tara and I were a married couple, with her being my secretary and me being an international exporter.

In fairness to Tara, I think it's appropriate to add a reminder here that the past was largely unfair to women, and the further we have to travel back in time, the more challenges she will encounter in playing her part. As a result, she will have to rein in her outgoing personality and remember that very few men will consider her an equal.

For this mission, Rodney provided Tara and me with conservative clothing that fit the times. That was something neither of us was thrilled about, but the fashions of the Roaring Twenties had yet to arrive.

Since we didn't expect any danger, we checked into what appeared to be one of Ottawa's best hotels and began asking around where we could find Duncan Campbell Scott. Because people at the time knew Duncan more for his poetry than for his efforts to assimilate indigenous people (we would have to call them *Indians* from now on), we decided that a proposal to bring

161

his poetry to far-flung areas would be the best way to approach him.

On the afternoon of our second day, we caught up with the stern-faced, bespectacled, fifty-seven-year-old man at a main street café. That meeting we arranged through the hotel proprietor, who was happy to set up the introduction in exchange for a generous tip.

The three of us sat at an out-of-the-way table, with Duncan across from me and Tara sitting silently by my side.

At first glance, Duncan struck me as a man you couldn't simply ask, "Hey, do you wanna come over to our hotel room tonight and get hammered?" On second and third glances, he also struck me as a man you couldn't simply ask, "Hey, do you wanna come over to our hotel room tonight and get hammered?"

So rather than do that, we stuck with our cover story and promised Duncan wealth and fame in Australia.

After introductions and some small talk, I took a long sip of tea and said to him, "Australians have a craving for poetry that I haven't seen elsewhere. That's especially the case in outback towns, where large groups get together on Saturday afternoons for poetry readings. Best of all, those people have never been exposed to high-quality outdoor-themed poetry like yours. The Jack London novels I've exported there are the closest comparisons I can think of. His wilderness adventures sell out the moment they leave the shipping dock. You could be poetry's Jack London!"

His dour expression brightened. "Do you really think so?"

"I'm telling you, Australians are gonna freak out when they read your poems!"

"Freak out?"

"Um . . . It's an Australian term that means *fall in love*."

I made a mental note to avoid using slang on this mission.

Our short meeting ended with an agreement to get together at my hotel room the following evening. At that time, Duncan would give to me a collection of his best unpublished poems, and I would give to him a contract and an advance payment. I didn't know how the publishing industry worked in present time, much less how it worked in the early 1900s, but I reasoned that as long as I spoke in an authoritative tone—like a right-wing radio host—Duncan would believe whatever bullshit I told him.

Apparently, it worked.

Chapter 26

The Racist Poet

After our second night in Ottawa, Tara and I decided that larger accommodations would be necessary for our important meeting with Duncan Campbell Scott. I walked down to the lobby and gave the proprietor enough cash to move us to his best room. That room, while not luxurious by modern standards, had a small, separate sitting area with a couch, coffee table, and writing desk. Then, with the help of Rodney doing research in present time, Tara hand-wrote two copies of a simple publishing agreement.

When Duncan arrived, Tara and I ushered him upstairs to our room and over to the sitting area. As soon as we took our seats, Duncan looked at me and asked, "Why is this woman joining us again? I thought tonight we would be engaging in man-talk."

I kept a straight face and said, "I apologize. Not only is she my wife and secretary, but tonight she's also our servant, here to provide us with anything we need."

He frowned and nodded acceptance.

"Would you like a cigar, sir?" Tara asked in a voice only I knew was sarcastic.

He forced a smile. "Yes. That would be fine."

"Very good, sir. I'll get a special one—just for you!"

While Tara walked down to the lobby to buy a cigar, I handed Duncan the contract to read over. He, in turn, handed me a folder containing a collection of his poems. I read a few of them, stopping after each one to tell him how wonderful I thought it was. In truth, I had trouble understanding how anyone could have considered him one of the great Canadian poets of his era. After all, this man wrote "Half-Breed Girl"—a poem that was every bit as ignorant as its title was.

Then again, Duncan's most famous quote as a representative of the Canadian government was, "I want to get rid of the Indian problem. I do not think as a matter of fact, that this country ought to continuously protect a class of people who are able to stand alone. That is my whole point. . . . Our object is to continue until there is not a single Indian in Canada that has not been absorbed into the body politic, and there is no Indian question, and no Indian department, that is the whole object of this Bill."

Even though the Canadian government eventually apologized to the indigenous people for the abuse and deaths caused by their assimilation program, Duncan's bigotry—both as a poet and as the deputy superintendent of the Department of Indian Affairs—represented the mainstream thinking of white Canadians during that time.

Knowing that, Duncan Campbell Scott certainly appeared to be the kind of person Ralph would choose to occupy. Not only would Duncan be predisposed to Ralph's goals, but he was also living among people who would provide little or no resistance. Whether or not Ralph was influencing him, the man sitting across from me disgusted me—and he was going down.

Tara returned and handed Duncan a cigar. "Would you like me to light that for you, sir?"

He leaned forward to receive the light, took a long puff, and said to me, "I accept the terms of your contract."

"Wonderful!" I replied. "And I accept these poems. I will have them printed and bound and on their way to Australia within six months. By this time next year, you'll be the most famous poet on the continent."

We took a moment to sign the contracts before I counted out Duncan's cash advance and set it on the table.

"I think this calls for a celebration!" Tara said in a bubbly voice.

"That's what the cigar is for," Duncan said.

"What if we had something even better than a cigar?" I asked.

"You are not suggesting . . . ?" He straightened his posture. "I am a government official, and drinking alcoholic beverages is prohibited!"

Tara set a whiskey bottle and three small glasses on the coffee table. "Are you a government official or a great poet? All the great ones drink. I remember when Jack London signed a similar Australian contract. Mister Westin offered him double or nothing on his advance if he could beat me in a drinking contest. Well . . . ," she shyly bowed her head. "I am just a lady, so Mister London walked away with quite a bit of money that night."

"Yeah, I'm never doin' that again." I laughed and looked Duncan in the eyes. "If she wasn't my wife, I would've taken all that she lost me out of her pay."

"Oh, come on," Tara begged. "Let me try again. I can do better this time."

"Mister Scott said no. Besides, Jack London was a novelist—a real man's man. Poets are made from different stock. You might actually win, and I'd like to see Mister Scott keep his advance."

Duncan glanced around the room before asking, "Double or nothing?"

I nodded and said, "Uh-huh."

He reached for a glass. "Lock the door!"

As Tara locked the door, I counted out a stack of bills equal to the previous one and set it on the table.

When she returned, I said, "Here are the rules. I will fill each glass one-third of the way up, and on my signal, you will each empty your glass in a single swallow. The contest ends when one of you fails to drink the entire contents, vomits, or falls asleep. Any questions?"

They both shook their heads.

I poured the first round. "Drink up!"

They downed their whiskeys and tried not to react to the burn.

I also poured myself a third of a glass and gulped it down. Rodney had given us some powerful whiskey! I stayed with Tara and Duncan for two more rounds. I did so not only to appear sporting, but also because I was curious to learn how much difference my refurbished liver would make. Although I could still feel the alcohol—no doubt about it—the overall buzz seemed to be about half of what I had experienced with my original liver.

When we moved on to the second bottle, I regretted drinking so much. What if we finished both bottles and Duncan was still awake? Another concern was that Tara was significantly smaller than her opponent. There was no guarantee she'd win.

I poured another round.

Tara downed her glass and slurred, "There once was a poet from Ottawa, who thought he could outdrink a lady from . . . from. What rhymes with Ottawa?"

"You were born in Missoula," I said while replenishing both glasses.

She swallowed her whiskey and tried again. "There once was a poet from Ottawa, who thought he could outdrink a lady from Missoula . . . la. But he was a dink, a racist fink, who ended up in the clink."

Marty Essen

Duncan scowled as he tried to utter a response. His head fell back, and he passed out.

"Where did you put the trap-capsules?" I asked.

"You're asking a drunk?" Tara replied. "I thought you had them."

We both stood—me much more steadily than her—and began a frantic search of the hotel room.

"Rodney!" I called out. "You've been with us the whole time. You must have seen where we placed them."

He materialized. "Sorry, I was multitasking again, and I do not always pay as close attention as I should when doing that. In fact, right now I am . . . well, you do not want to know."

I cringed. "Wait! Doesn't your customer service department record everything for quality and training purposes?"

"They only do that intermittently, now that I am a full-time planetary consultant, second class. I can check to see if the recent events were recorded, but before I do that, have you checked your pockets?"

"Of course," I said. "Twice."

"Check them again."

I reached inside one pocket after the other. "Oh, here they are! I swear they weren't there a minute ago."

I returned to the sitting area to find Duncan with his head back and mouth open—snoring away. I tossed a capsule into his mouth and pushed his jaw closed. "Now, Rodney!"

Rodney flashed out and back. "Sorry," he said slowly. "No Ralph."

"Damn!"

"If you would like to use your credit now, I can send Duncan to the depository planet."

I paused to think. "No, Tara made up a poem that gave me a better idea." I looked into the bedroom. My lover was curled up on the bed—fast asleep. "But I'm gonna let her nap for a bit first."

168

* * *

While Tara and Duncan slept, I walked down to the front desk to get the directions necessary to put my plan into action. An hour later, I poured Tara a cup of coffee and said, "Wake up, sleepyhead. We have work to do."

I waited for her to finish her coffee before glancing out our window. With no taverns to serve alcohol, Ottawa had quieted down quickly after dark. It was time to go. Tara grabbed the half-finished second bottle of whiskey, and I rolled Duncan into a large rug and hoisted him onto my shoulder. We descended the rear stairway and exited onto the dirt road behind the hotel. From there, Tara served as my lookout as I carried Duncan six or so blocks to the street where the police station was located.

I took a moment to scan up and down the street before deciding that directly in front of the police station was too obvious. Instead, I unrolled the deputy superintendent of the Department of Indian Affairs a half-block away, propped him into a sitting position, poured just enough whiskey onto his clothing to make sure he smelled, and set the bottle between his legs.

After that, it was just a simple matter of popping my head inside the front door of the police station and reporting a passed-out drunk down the street.

Once we returned to the hotel, I began worrying that the police might give a man of Duncan's stature a pass. Alerting the press would make sure that didn't happen. Our room lacked a phone, so I used the candlestick phone in the lobby. In present time, reaching the editor of a newspaper after hours might be difficult. In 1919, all I had to do was ask the operator to connect me to the home of the editor of the *Ottawa Journal,* and she put me right through.

The last decision we had to make was whether to move to a different hotel, in case Duncan ratted us out. Ultimately, we decided to dispose of the glasses and the empty whiskey bottle and take our chances where we were. If the police showed up, we'd deny having ever met Duncan. If the police arrested us, we'd simply escape later the next morning, when our time travel window opened up.

We returned to present time without incident.

* * *

After settling back in at the cabin and taking a moment to grab a snack, I booted up my laptop computer and searched the internet for Duncan Campbell Scott. As had been the case since Rodney came into my life, there was good news and bad news. The good news was that Duncan had spent a short time in jail for public drunkenness and lost his job as the deputy superintendent of the Department of Indian Affairs. The bad news was that his replacement—a person strongly recommended by the leaders of all the churches involved in residential schools—had handled his position virtually the same way as Duncan had prior to the timeline change. At least six thousand indigenous children still died, and many times that number suffered horrific abuse.

As for Duncan's poetry career: it floundered for a few years after his arrest but flourished when prohibition ended. Apparently, repulsive poetry is impervious to timeline changes.

Chapter 27

Over Budget

T ara and I were cooling off with some soft drinks after a vigorous run with Clarice, when I called out from the kitchen table, "Rodney, are you multitasking again, or can I speak with you for a moment?"

He materialized, wearing a big smile. "I am always at your service, Stefan."

"So far, we've visited the three locations in the dreams you sent to Tara, but not the three locations in the dreams you sent to me. If I remember correctly, my three dreams took place on a plantation in the South during slavery, in Salem during the witch trials, and in Spain during the Spanish Inquisition."

"That is correct."

"Considering that during both of our encounters with Ralph, he practically begged us to meet him in Salem, I have two time travel suggestions for you that both involve skipping the South during slavery."

"Okay, but first tell me why you want to skip the South."

"I want to skip it because the people there who used the Bible to justify slavery are too numerous to narrow down. How are you going to pick Ralph out of all those clergymen and slaveholders? Or what if Ralph was influencing a Confederate general, like Robert E. Lee or Stonewall Jackson? On top of that, there's no way Tara and I will be able to resist the chance to use our special abilities to free some slaves and kick some slaveholder ass. Those slaveholders had guns, and as far as I know, the refurbished skin you gave us isn't bulletproof. It's not very superhero of me, but if you send us into the South during slavery, we probably won't come back alive."

"Then what alternatives do you propose?"

"Either send us directly to Salem or, better yet, forget about the hazards of jumping too far into the past and send us directly to the time of Christ. Obviously, we know Ralph will be there. He won't even have to see us. We can simply slip a trap-capsule into an olive before Jesus eats it and catch Ralph without a confrontation."

Rodney frantically pushed out his hands. "No! No! You cannot go to the time of Christ!"

"Why?" Tara and I asked in unison.

"Because if we are successful at capturing Ralph, my people intend to punish him for what he has done. If you grab him too early, none of what he did will have happened, and he can claim innocence."

"But wouldn't that be better for all of us here on Earth?" Tara asked. "Think of all the lives he destroyed that will be restored. And need I remind you that you got Stefan and me involved in this project to save our planet from environmental destruction? From our point of view, capturing Ralph any time before he influences the unholy marriage between conservative Christians and anti-environmental Republicans is much more important than enabling the punishment of an individual. Also, with Ralph out of the way from the beginning, us humans will have a chance to evolve a common set of ethics with less outside influence—and we just might be better off for it."

I nodded and added, "Didn't you say earlier that your people feel responsible for planting the seed that started all of this? Then why don't you let us remove that seed before it has a chance to germinate?"

Once again, Rodney retrieved his virtual chair and sat. "Stefan, do you agree with all the laws in your country?"

"No."

"Tara, how about you?"

"No."

"But you follow them anyway."

"Generally," she said. "I've been known to exceed the speed limit from time to time."

"Then you will understand that, in this instance, I agree with you. Grabbing Ralph before he leaves the body known as Jesus Christ is the best way to go. Unfortunately, at the same time my people banned in-person travel *to* your planet, they also banned time travel *on* your planet to any period prior to when Ralph made his second body switch. They anticipated this subject would eventually come up and wanted to make sure Ralph could not escape without punishment."

"Why do your people get to make the rules for our planet?" Tara asked.

"If you can come up with a way to travel to the time of Jesus without our help—go for it! The rules I have mentioned only apply to my people. That said, I could not send you to a forbidden time even if I wanted to, because those much higher than me would immediately reject such a request."

"Where does all this leave us?" I asked.

"Hold on."

Rodney disappeared just long enough for Tara to grab a brush to work on some burs caught in Clarice's fur and for me to grab a treat to bribe the dog to stay still.

When Rodney reappeared, he sat on the edge of his chair and said, "I have discussed our situation with my supervisor. She reminded me that time travel is expensive and that the seven jumps we have engaged in have already put us over budget. Therefore—"

"We've only time traveled four times," I interrupted. "Massachusetts, Brazil, Italy, and Canada."

"Plus the three jumps, so you could take your chloroquine pills."

"Those count?" I asked.

"When it comes to the budget, all time travels matter."

"That sucks!" Tara blurted. "Stefan and I would've been happy to delay the Brazil trip by two weeks, but you couldn't wait. On top of that, we had Ralph caught in Italy and only lost him because of Fluffy's incompetence."

"If you will let me finish." He folded his arms and huffed. "Therefore, my supervisor was happy with your suggestion to eliminate a trip to the South during slavery. In fact, for a moment she even considered declaring the entire project a lost cause and moving ahead with the planet recycling. Then I reminded her about what happened with Fluffy, and she agreed to add one more jump."

"What about the three unnecessary Montana time jumps you sent us on?" I asked.

"I could not bring those up. She knows about them, of course. But in the mood she was in, a reminder would have likely gotten me fired, or at least reassigned. And do you know who would have taken my place if that happened?"

"Fluffy," I said.

"Fluffy," he repeated. "But I am still not finished. I also convinced my supervisor to add an additional time jump in exchange for the deportation credits both of you have for your skin. That is it, unfortunately. We either succeed in two tries or the Earth gets recycled."

"Will those final tries be to Salem during the witch trials and to Spain during the Inquisition?" I asked.

"I think we all agree that Salem has to be next on our list, but if we get down to a final time jump, it is only fair that I leave that destination up to you and Tara."

"You obviously know more about Ralph and have more advanced research tools than Tara and I have. If we reach that do-or-die trip, will you still provide us with guidance?"

"Absolutely! I will do whatever research is necessary."

"Good," I said. "Send us to Salem tomorrow. Until then, Tara and I would love some time alone to relax and get a solid night's sleep. If you want something to keep you busy while we're doing that, I have someone for you to research."

"Who?"

"Christopher Columbus."

Rodney's chair morphed into a witch's broom. He flew several laps around the inside of my head before waving and shouting, "I will check out Columbus while you rejuvenate. So long!"

He disappeared through the side of my head.

Chapter 28

Like Wild Animals

T ara and I planned to arrive in Salem Village on July 16, 1692, three days before five people were to be hanged for witchery. We selected that date, because we wanted to make sure some good came out of our journey. If we couldn't catch Ralph, we could at least kick some Puritan ass before the executions and then disappear. Yeah, disappearing in front of everyone would really fuck up their minds.

Then again, disappearing in front of everyone might actually increase the number of people executed for being witches. We'd have to think about that one and decide what to do when the time came.

Coming up with a cover story for this mission was a bit of a challenge. I originally suggested that I could be a newspaper reporter with Tara as my assistant, but newspapers wouldn't become a thing until the 1700s. Well, technically, a newspaper in Boston was published in 1690, but that paper lasted for only a single issue. We ultimately elected to reprise our roles as a doctor and nurse, this time from Boston.

Another problem we would encounter was where to stay. Just

as we were too early for newspapers, we were also too early for hotels. Fortunately, Rodney had an answer for that, with camping gear that would fit inside large hidden pockets built into the period-appropriate clothing he had provided us.

While Tara and I looked through the supplies that had suddenly appeared on my kitchen table, Rodney elaborated. "The TITTS treaty strictly forbids weapons or luggage on time jumps, but it does not specify how much storage capacity time travelers can build into their clothing. Some travelers abuse that loophole with clothing that is much more outrageous than what I have given you. In front of you are supplies for a three-to four-day camping trip, including food tablets, a water purifier, a tent, a stove, a first aid kit, and bedding. Most of the supplies are technologically superior to what you have on present day Earth, and all are compact enough to fit into your pockets."

"Why didn't you offer us similar items before?" Tara asked.

"The only place where they could have been beneficial to you was in Brazil. There, however, you were going directly into a village, where I expected you would find lodging. On this jump, I think it will be safer for you to set up camp outside the village and make day trips in. Beyond that, the main reason I did not give you similar supplies on previous trips is that bringing such items adds some danger."

"Danger?" she asked.

"Yes. That is because of our strict 'leave no trace' policy. Imagine how leaving advanced technology behind could affect a timeline. Therefore, except for your supply of trap-capsules, which qualify for remote retrieval, you must bring back every item that features technology that is noticeably beyond the period you are visiting. All such items are tagged before you make your time jump. If even one of those items is missing, all return time jump attempts will automatically be rejected until every item is accounted for."

"Can't you just grab the items separately?" I asked.

"Sure, technically, but for security reasons, the TITTS treaty specifically requires all returning time travelers to have in their direct possession every advanced item they departed with."

"What happens if something gets lost or stolen?" I asked.

"I will hope that you enjoy living in 1692," he replied.

* * *

Our time jump landed us at the edge of a forest, on the outskirts of Salem Village. I peered through the trees and could see a dirt road and several small houses.

"Rodney," I said. "Can you be our virtual GPS and keep us from getting lost?"

"Sure."

I glanced behind me. "Good, the possibility of being stuck in 1692 kind of frightens me. I want to head straight back into the woods, two or three miles, and set up camp there. If you can lead us to a small open area next to a spring or a creek, you'll be an interplanetary hero."

"And if that open area features a soft, flat bed of moss to pitch our tent on, you'll be an interplanetary *superhero*," Tara added.

"I will do my best," he said.

Our hike took us into a forest of pine and birch, where the undergrowth was sparse enough that we could walk without feeling the need to bushwhack. After a few minutes, Tara waved a hand in front of her face and asked, "Rodney, do we have any high-tech bug dope with us?"

"Actually, the solution you requested is low tech. A natural repellent is included in your food tablets. Eat one, and within an hour, no biting insect will want to be within three feet of you."

"What about me?" I asked. "We're gonna be sleeping in the same tent."

Rodney didn't have his visual image on at the time, but I could hear the smile in his voice when he said, "I think there will be multiple times during this mission when you will be thankful that you do not have a refurbished nose."

* * *

Forty minutes later, Tara proclaimed, "Rodney, you're a superhero! This looks perfect."

Not only did we have a soft, flat spot where we could set up our camp, but we also had access to clean water that bubbled up from a spring a short distance away.

I had to ask, "Rodney, when this is all over with, can I summon you when I go backpacking in the mountains? A living GPS that can find geological features no one else knows exist is a true nature-lover's superpower."

"I am not authorized to answer that at this time," he said.

"Aw, I thought we'd moved beyond such secrecy."

"Sorry."

I pulled the tent out of a bag barely large enough to hold a sandwich, and it instantly expanded and set itself up. "Rodney, this is so cool! Can I at least keep the tent?"

"I am not authorized to answer that at this time," he repeated.

"Damn!"

Once we had everything in place for a comfortable stay in the woods, Tara asked, "Hey, Rodney, do you think we'll be safe leaving all this up when we hike into the village? As compact as everything is, it's still a lot to carry around in our pockets."

"I do not know much more than you do," he said. "My guess is that there is little chance of any Puritans coming out here, because they are afraid of the indigenous people."

"But the indigenous people could find our camp," I said to Tara before looking up to talk to our intergalactic handler, as had become my habit. "Rodney, I suggest you use some of your multi-tasking time to learn whatever languages the tribes here use."

My upward gaze gave me an idea. Overlooking our campsite was an old oak tree, with its lowest branch roughly fifteen feet off the ground. And just above that branch, the trunk had a hole in it. With my original legs, I could barely jump high enough to touch a ten-foot basketball rim. What could I do with my refurbished legs? There was only one way to find out. I crouched slightly before springing into the air.

The angle of my jump was perfect—to land belly-first atop the branch. "Ouch!" I squeaked out as I gasped for breath. Yes, my abdomen was most definitely all original.

Tara laughed. "What are you doing up there?"

I pulled myself all the way up onto the branch before answering, "I wanna check out the hole in this tree." I scooted over and looked into the dark hollow. Well, dark for someone without enhanced eyesight. Inside, I could see the remains of an old nest. It would be perfect.

I jumped down. "We can fit all the high-tech items into the hole before we head to the village."

Disappointment washed over Tara's face. "We just set up camp. Now you want to tear it down?"

"No. I'm all for hanging out here for the rest of the day and using our enhanced hearing and eyesight after dark to determine if we're near the paths of any indigenous people or large animals. I'll sleep much better once I'm reasonably confident we won't be in for a rude awakening."

"And that will move us one day closer to our time travel window."

"That too."

* * *

Other than our runs with Clarice, Tara and I had had little opportunity to explore our new abilities while not under duress. That I was capable of jumping onto a branch fifteen feet in the air was something I should have known a long time ago. And it made me wonder, what if Tara and I got into a situation that required a twenty-foot jump? Could we do it?

That night we took to the forest like wild animals. We ran as fast as we could, jumped as high as we could, and tested our strength by throwing rocks and breaking branches. We also tested our hearing by trying to sneak up on each other. While all those powers were exciting to have, what I enjoyed most was the ability to see at night. The freedom to run through the dark woods like a wolf was exhilarating!

On the negative side, I remembered watching reruns of *The Six Million Dollar Man* as a child and wondering how Steve Austin could lift a car without a bionic back. My childhood question proved accurate. Even though my arms and legs were tremendously strong, I still had the back of a thirty-eight-year-old doctor. Lifting a standard-sized car would likely be unrealistic, but if I could master the coordination, I could probably enjoy a brief career in baseball as the first pitcher with a fastball that exceeded one hundred ten miles per hour.

We wrapped up our evening, confident that other than a black bear who wanted no part of humans, we could go to sleep without worrying about unwanted visitors in the middle of the night.

Chapter 29

Manipulated for Nefarious Purposes

In the morning, Tara and I checked around to make sure no one was watching us, packed up all our high-tech camping gear, and stuffed it into the hole in the tree.

Since we were going to be on the move, our planetary consultant was in verbal mode when I called out to him, "Rodney, are you sure you can get us back to this campsite again?"

"Yes. Today, you only need to worry about finding Ralph."

As we began our hike to the village, Tara said, "Rodney, all I know about Salem during the time of the witch trials and hangings is what I learned in a high school history class and the little we discussed before making this jump. I've been assuming that Reverend Samuel Parris is our target, but others, such as William Stoughton, are also possibilities. Can you please give us a preview of what to expect?"

"Reverend Samuel Parris is most definitely your target." He materialized, holding a framed portrait of Parris. "Without him, the Salem witch trials and hangings would not have happened. The entire historic episode is classic Ralph. Not only was he easily able to manipulate Samuel Parris as his primary subject, but he also manipulated more than half the residents in the village as secondary subjects. Historians have never been able to explain with certainty the bizarre behavior of the children who accused others of witchery, including Parris's own daughter, Betty. What caused their catatonic states and fits of possession? Was it child abuse? Was it encephalitis? Was it epilepsy? Was it LSD-like hallucinations from the fungus ergot in their rye bread?"

I raised my hand like a child in grade school. "I know! I know!" Rodney called on me. "Stefan?"

"It was Ralph, jumping from person to person."

"Exactly! And that is why he was so eager to confront you here. Since he has easy access to so many people, he could be occupying any of them at any particular time. And because he knows these people well, he could even be directing them with the equivalent of a post-hypnotic suggestion to continue his goals after he departs their bodies. Keep that in mind, if you find yourself in a fight with multiple people. Ralph could be controlling all of them to various degrees, jumping from person to person when necessary and leaving suggestions with those he finds most malleable."

"How many people live in Salem Village?" Tara asked.

"Roughly five hundred fifty," Rodney said. "But you could end up visiting two locations during this jump. Samuel Parris, the girls who made the accusations, and the initial people accused of witchery all lived in Salem Village. The trials and the hangings took place five miles to the south in Salem Town, which at the time was roughly three times larger than the village. Do not expect to see a trial today, since the hangings will take place tomorrow. Instead, your goal is to find Samuel Parris at his parsonage or his church, making final preparations for his trip to Salem Town."

Rodney turned off his visual image, and we walked silently the rest of the way to the village.

* * *

Even though Tara and I were dressed as Puritans, blending in was impossible in a village where everyone knew everybody. As we followed the main dirt road past houses, people stared at us from their windows and doorways, and children doing outside chores stopped what they were doing to run inside.

Our virtual GPS told us that all we needed to do was continue down the road and we would run right into the church. Although I wasn't particularly nervous, the village felt creepy—and way too quiet. The only sounds were an occasional birdcall and the *thunk* of someone chopping wood.

When we reached the church, I asked, "Rodney, are you gonna help us with seventeenth century English, or should we just wing it?"

"I will do my best to give you an accent appropriate for the time and location. I will also try to prevent you from using words that do not yet exist."

"Yeah, I imagine some of our vocabulary would elicit a blank stare."

We opened the door to the church and stepped inside. Based on the body odor that assaulted us, I would have expected all the pews to be full. Instead, the only person inside was a slump-shouldered old woman sweeping the floor.

She looked at us and asked, "Are you seeking the Reverend Parris?"

"Yes," I said. "Do you know where we might find him?"

"He was here a moment ago. He probably went to fetch something at his parsonage. You can wait for him here if you like."

We sat in the nearest pew and looked around. The rectangular two-story building was as plain on the inside as it was on the outside. It had none of the stained glass windows, high ceilings, or crosses that you'd see in a modern church. Mostly, it was a dark, smelly, wooden box.

A few minutes later, a man who appeared to be about my age, with a hooked nose and brown, shoulder-length hair, entered through the rear door.

Tara and I stood.

"Reverend Parris?" I asked.

"Yes?"

"I'm Doctor Stefan Westin, from Boston, and this is my wife Tara."

He scowled. "Have you come to examine the afflicted? Or are you just outsiders, coming to stick your noses into business that doesn't concern you?"

"May the love of Jesus bless you too!" Tara replied.

His face softened. "I'm sorry. Every time someone new arrives, I must assume Satan has sent him."

"Paranoid much?" she blurted.

Rodney materialized and shook a finger. "Sorry, I was not fast enough to mute you, Tara, but you are at least two hundred years too early to use that word." He disappeared.

She tried again. "You say *him*, but aren't most of the witches here women?"

His expression grew confused. "I don't see how the two are related. A minion from hell, sent by Satan, would take the form of a strong man. That's different from when Satan leads someone into witchery. Women are more sinful and weaker in the body and in the head than men are, and therefore easier for Satan to possess."

I put a hand on Tara's shoulder and whispered, "Let it go."

She brushed off my hand. "Sinful? It seems to me that the only one being sinful here is a *man* accusing multiple innocent women of witchery to raise his own status in the village."

Samuel trembled as he pointed a finger, inches from Tara's nose. "Witch!"

"I've been called a bitch before, but never a witch. Hmm . . . I kind of like it. But if you don't take that finger out of my face, this weak, sinful woman is gonna beat the living shit out of you."

He continued pointing as he screamed, "Witch! *Witch!*"

Tara's hand flashed faster than a viper strike. She grabbed Samuel by the wrist, twisted his arm behind him, and slammed his head to the floor as her free hand whooshed from the opposite side and jammed a trap-capsule into his ear! "Rodney, now!"

The slump-shouldered woman looked up from her sweeping and said, "Nice move, but no one here speaks like you do."

Tara reached down and pulled the trap-capsule from the dazed reverend's ear. "I knew I shouldn't have used the word *shit!*"

"No, shit is perfectly acceptable. You just can't wear the clothing of a weak Puritan woman and then come on strong."

Tara smiled and held out a hand. "How's it going, Ralph?"

He ignored her offer to shake. "Ralph? I hate that name! Call me Jesus."

"No. I like Ralph," she said.

He waved the slump-shouldered woman's hand dismissively and said, "It doesn't matter. Despite your obvious strength, it will do you little good when you're vastly outnumbered." Through the woman's eyes, he regarded the crumpled body on the floor. "I assume whatever you removed from his ear was designed to capture me."

"Yes."

"Can I see it?"

Tara held it up.

"Set it on the floor and smash it with your shoe."

She did as he said.

"I'm going to return to Samuel Parris now. This old body is full of aches and pains." The slump-shouldered woman sank into a pew. The reverend, apparently still dazed, did not move, however.

Tara and I looked at each other with wide eyes.

"Did he leave without saying 'toodle-oo'?" I asked.

"Apparently so."

"Well, you blew that one! You couldn't just ease into the mission? Get to know Samuel; gain his confidence; free some witches; that sort of thing."

"I'm sorry. He pissed me off."

The back door opened, and a dark-haired girl who appeared to be about ten stepped inside. She pointed a gun at us.

"A musket?" Tara asked. "No one told me there'd be guns."

"It's a Second Amendment model," I said.

"What?"

"The kind of gun the Founding Fathers had in mind when they wrote the Second Amendment."

"Yeah, I imagine it would be tough to shoot up a school with one of those."

"But it could kill one of us."

The girl aimed the gun at Tara before swinging it toward me. "Up against the wall!" she demanded in a mature voice.

She waited for us to follow her instructions. Then she handed the gun to Samuel Parris, who instantly recovered. The reverend stood and said to the girl, "Betty! Go find Thomas Putnam. Tell him to come right away and bring some friends."

As Betty departed, Ralph/Samuel held his gun on us. "Is this the first time we've met?"

"No," I said.

"Oh, good. That means I've already won at least one round."

I leaned against the wall as casually as I could and asked, "Do you really believe all this witch bullshit, or is it just an act?"

"If we've met before, you already know the answer to that question. While my specialty is Christianity, it really doesn't matter what the religion is. Once you indoctrinate the masses, you can manipulate them. Even those who are otherwise decent will commit the most horrific acts if they believe it is in service of their god. I'm sure you're aware of my work during the Spanish Inquisition."

"Of course."

"Here in Salem Village, I'm demonstrating that leaving the Catholic Church and moving to a new land changes nothing. Any form of Christianity can be manipulated for nefarious purposes."

"There must be another way to make your point," I said.

He grimaced. "Humans tortured me on a cross, when all I was doing was bringing them a message to love one another! Your vile species will pay for that crime as long as I occupy this planet."

"Why didn't you just move to another body before Jesus was crucified?" Tara asked.

"Traveling between bodies is a skill that must be learned. Up to that point, I had only occupied a single body, so I expected my people to grab me before the first spike pierced Jesus's wrist. When that didn't happen, I was stuck inside his body until he died. In fact, it was longer than that. I was trapped in the corpse for three days before I figured out that temporarily reanimating it would allow me to escape and travel between bodies."

"That must have been horrible," Tara said.

"Sympathy will do you no good—human!"

A horse whinnied as a wagon pulled up in front of the church. Five men rushed in. One, I assumed, was Thomas Putnam.

Ralph/Samuel pointed with his gun. "Satan sent these two to infest our village. Lock them up until they stand trial!"

One of the men stepped outside. He returned with four pairs of shackles.

"Restrain the woman first," Ralph/Samuel demanded. "She's more dangerous than she looks."

Rodney flashed in. "Do not let them shackle you!"

"We can just time jump out when the window opens," Tara replied, not caring who heard her.

"You cannot time travel without first securing the technology hidden in the tree!" He flashed out.

"Shit!" Tara kicked one man halfway across the church and was about to do serious damage to another when a click from the gun's flintlock made her freeze.

I froze too and released the headlocks I had on two men.

Ralph/Samuel stood with the business end of his musket inches away from my forehead. He pointed to the men with his chin and said, "Finish shackling the woman. And Thomas, find another musket."

"There's one in the wagon," said a well-built man, now confirmed as Thomas Putnam.

As Thomas stepped out the door, I considered my options. Should I call upon the coordination of Jackie Chan or should I run like a dog?

My thoughts were cut short when Thomas returned sooner than expected.

Fighting six men, two armed with muskets, seemed like poor odds—especially for Tara, who was already in restraints. Instead, I swept an arm up and knocked Ralph/Samuel's musket toward the ceiling. Somehow, he held on, but that was all I needed. I slipped through the hands of the other men and darted out the back door!

The men pursued, but they were no match for my speed.

Once I was sure no one was following me, I looked up and said, "Rodney, I feel like a cowardly shit for what I just did."

He materialized and replied, "Now that you and Tara are separated, I have turned off conference mode to avoid confusion. And if you would like my opinion, running was the correct decision."

"Tell Tara, I'll be back."

"Would you like me to tell her in my voice or in Arnold Schwarzenegger's voice?"

"Arnold's. She could use a laugh right about now."

Rodney did his disappeary-reappeary thing. "She says not to beat yourself up over it, and that she has always wanted to be saved by a terminator in shining armor."

"Where is she now?"

"In the back of the wagon, on the way to the Salem Town jail."

"Can you track her and lead me to the tree at the same time?"

"Sure. Multitasking is kind of my thing."

"If you want a third item to keep you occupied, come up with a plan for me."

"Already done. It is time for you to take full advantage of your enhanced eyesight and hearing. Tonight, those senses will give you a tremendous advantage over anyone at the jail who is guarding Tara."

"I like that. Get me to the tree and then to the jail."

Chapter 30

Don't Underestimate the Lice

U pon my arrival at the tree, I filled a flexible container with water and retrieved the high-tech camping supplies. After stuffing all the items into my pockets, I called out, "Rodney, before I depart, can you confirm that I have everything?"

Since it would have been distracting for him to loiter inside my brain, looking at who knows what while I was hiking, Rodney had reverted to verbal mode and responded that way. "Congratulations! You have not missed a thing."

"How's Tara doing?"

"She is still in the back of the wagon—hurling insults at everyone. In present time, Tara stands out. Here, she is far beyond anything the men guarding her have ever experienced. She is simultaneously frightening and enchanting them—and one appears ready to commit suicide."

"Oh, I can relate." I started running in what felt like a southerly direction before double-checking with my in-head navigator. "Which way?"

"Go straight for now. I will tell you when to turn."

"Hey, Rodney."

"Yes."

"Doesn't it seem strange to you that Reverend Samuel Parris has the power to send someone to jail?"

"Legally, he does not. A magistrate will have to sign off on Tara's arrest, but that is merely a technicality. Remember that you are in Massachusetts Bay Colony, not the United States of America. Here, as in many other societies throughout history, clergy have way more authority than they should have. Since the people in this colony believe in witches, who better to point one out than a Puritan preacher?"

"What happens if I fail to break Tara out of jail?"

"She will have to prove her innocence in a trial. That trial will be humiliating and include being forced to strip naked in front of the court, where every inch of her will be examined for witch's marks."

"So the Puritans were sexual molesters! Why am I not surprised?"

I ran in silence for a while before it occurred to me that running was unnecessary. Darkness was still hours away, and Ralph/Samuel would have people looking for me. My best bet was to slink along in the forest, with Rodney on standby to let me know if serious danger ever threatened Tara. Should that happen, I could turn on the speed and reach her quickly.

A few miles later, Rodney broke the silence. "Tara is now inside the jail. They left her shackles on and put her directly into the basement dungeon with the rest of the alleged witches."

"The Salem jail has a dungeon?"

"Yeah, I thought that strange too. I checked, and in present time you can even visit a museum with a replica of that dungeon."

"Holy shit. Is Tara holding up okay?"

"She says the conditions are overcrowded and appalling.

Everything smells like rancid shit; some of the women are near death; lice infest everyone, and rats are scurrying about. Oh, and she has dibs on the first shower when you get home."

* * *

The sun was low in the sky when I spotted the wood-sided two-story jail, near what Rodney had identified as the North River. I stopped to observe from a distance. Two men with muskets were standing outside the building, engaged in conversation, and four women were kneeling at the doorstep, praying.

"Rodney, can you conference me in with Tara, so I can talk with her directly?"

He materialized. "Not directly. But remember in Brazil, when I gave you the play-by-play between Tara and Wesley? I can do the same here. You will both hear me imitating the other's voice."

"Good enough. Inform Tara."

He flashed out and returned a moment later. "She is ready."

My voice: "Hi hon. How are you holding up?"

Tara's voice (sarcastic): "When I'm eighty and looking back at my life, this will certainly be the highlight I'll remember that brought me the greatest joy."

My voice: "I am so sorry."

Tara's voice: "You have nothing to be sorry for. Had you stayed and fought, one or both of us might be dead right now."

My voice: "Have you tried breaking your shackles?"

Tara's voice: "Of course! I might stand a chance if I had something to give me leverage. The only inanimate objects down here are smooth rock walls and a dirt floor. Actually, the floor is more shit than dirt."

My voice: "Have you had a chance to talk with any of your cellmates?"

Tara's voice: "They haven't exactly warmed up to me. And I don't blame them. No one wants another person added to an already packed dungeon. One woman, however, did tell me to expect a visit from William Dounton."

My voice: "Who's he?"

Tara's voice: "I don't know. Hold on while I ask. *Hey! Can anyone in here tell me who William Dounton is?*"

I moved closer to the jail as I waited.

Tara's voice: "William Dounton is the jailer. He was the man who locked me in here. He gave me the creeps when he looked me up and down. Apparently, he reserves the most appealing prisoners for himself and trades out access to those women after he's finished with them. Most women receive a visit on their first night, while they're still relatively clean and healthy."

My voice: "And by access you mean—"

Tara's voice (interrupting): "Yes. Although I wouldn't worry too much about that. Shackles or not, I'll rip the balls off any man that touches me."

My voice: "I had planned to wait until everyone had fallen asleep before breaking you out. Now, I'll be ready to strike sooner. If at any time you're in danger from anything larger than a louse, let me know, and I'll be there in an instant."

Tara's voice: "Don't underestimate the lice. If I could train them to eat iron, I'd be out of here in no time. Hold on, the smell is really getting to me. I think I'm gonna . . . *throw up*."

My voice: "Are you okay?"

Tara's voice (retching): "Yeah, I've never . . . Hold on again. . . . *Bah!* Okay, I think I'm done for now. *Hey! Does anyone in here have a breath mint?*"

My voice: "How are your cellmates reacting to you talking to me?"

Tara's voice: "Oh, I think they're convinced that I'm the one genuine witch in here."

My voice: "I think my talking is attracting a bit of attention, too. There are two men in front of the jail, staring at me. I'm gonna move on and come back after dark. Contact me if you need me sooner."

Tara's voice: "I will."

Chapter 31

Don't Kill Abe!

I retreated into the forest, chewed some food tablets, and tried to take a nap. Indulging in such a break, knowing my lover was crammed into a rank dungeon, produced a guilt worthy of a visit to a Catholic priest. Nevertheless, a little rest would help me maintain my energy and stay alert when I needed it the most.

I must have fallen asleep, because the sound of Rodney imitating Tara's voice in the dark jolted me bolt upright.

Tara's voice: "Stefan! Now would be a good time to be that terminator in shining armor. I can hear several men's voices upstairs. I'm pretty sure they're bidding on me—and the bidding isn't for just one winner. It's for multiple winners and the order they get me. I can fight off one man while in shackles, but despite my earlier bravado, the odds aren't in my favor if they all attack at once."

My voice: "I'm on my way!"

I broke into a run.

"Stop!" Rodney shouted.

"What!"

"You have half of the high-tech camping gear in your pockets and left the other half on the ground. Bury all of it, now! Otherwise the gear will end up spread all over the place, and you will never escape 1692."

"I don't have time!"

"Yes, you do. Those are not normal fingers and fingernails you will be digging with. Dig like a dog, and you will be on your way in two minutes."

With no time to argue, I did as he said. My fingers sliced open a two-foot-deep hole. I dropped in all the gear, returned the dirt, and was on my way.

"See!" Rodney said. "You were even faster than I predicted."

Back running at top speed, I asked between breaths, "Are you sure I put everything into the hole?"

"You are good."

"Keep me connected with Tara."

"I am doing that automatically."

"Are you ready to give me Jackie Chan's fighting ability?"

"Are you sure you do not want Bruce Lee's instead? Tara was right about him being the better fighter."

"No! Stick with Jackie Chan. I know how it feels, and if anyone lays a hand on Tara, the only fighting ability I will need is Stefan Westin's!"

Earlier in the evening, as I was mentally preparing for the jail-break, I envisioned myself going all James Bond—stealthily taking out one man at a time and dragging him out of sight.

Fuck stealth!

I plowed into the half-asleep guards out front, used them as a battering ram to break down the door, and flung their muskets into the darkness. I ran inside and searched for the entrance to the dungeon.

My voice: "Tara! Where are you?"

Tara's voice: "Go left, down the hallway, and take the stairs to the basement. Down there, you'll see another hallway. Follow it to the dungeon door."

With no artificial lighting to guide me, my enhanced eyesight came in handy. I couldn't see in total darkness, but the glassless windows both upstairs and downstairs let in enough light from the sliver of a moon that I could see where I was going.

I reached my destination within seconds. An iron bar secured the wooden door, and a lock held the bar in place.

Fuck the iron bar!

I kicked through the door, opening a shoe-sized hole. Two more kicks allowed me to stick my head inside. I was just about to announce, "Here's Johnny!" in my best Jack Nicholson voice, when the smell hit me.

I retched!

And retched again.

The click of a flintlock froze me before I could go for a third.

"Back away from the door!" a gruff voice ordered. "No sudden movements."

I raised my hands and turned to face five men squeezed into the narrow hallway. In the rear were two men holding knives; in front of them was a man holding a lantern; and in front of him were two men holding muskets at my eye level.

"Who are you!" demanded the tallest man with a musket.

"Who are you?" I asked in return.

"William Dounton, the jailer. Now answer my question."

"Oh, William Dounton! I've heard about you. I'm Doctor Stefan Westin, and I'm just stopping by to pick up my girlfriend, Tara. We'll be out of your hair soon."

"She's kind of tied up at the moment," he said.

I tilted my head and looked him in the eyes. *"Puritan humor? Ralph, is that you?"*

"Shut up!"

"Oh, it *is* you! Do your buddies know you're the only witch here?"

"I said shut up!"

"You're right. Fuck this conversation!"

With the coordination of Jackie Chan and the speed of Doctor Refurb, I knocked one gun away with a kick and the other with a chop. Both guns fired as they hit the ground. I ignored the pain to my sensitive ears and went for the man with the lantern. A quick punch to his throat forced him to release his grip. I caught the lantern before it hit the ground and carefully blew it out.

Everything went black.

But not for me!

At first, five against one in the dark seemed like a fair fight, but each time I'd knock all the men unconscious they'd recover one by one and come at me again. Somehow, Ralph could revive whichever body he switched to. It was like fighting zombies! I was beginning to tire, when I changed tactics and went for their knees. Even zombies can't walk with their knees bent backward.

But that didn't stop Ralph. The men continued their attack—crawling toward me—only to fly against the back wall when I'd deliver a kick to their face. Now I was actually feeling sorry for the men. When this was all over, their mangled bodies would take months to recover—if they recovered at all.

Suddenly, the assault stopped. Ralph disappeared without even a toodle-oo.

I took a deep breath and broke the rest of the way into the dungeon. Where was Tara? I had expected to see her right away, but with so little light filtering in from the outside, and more prisoners in the dungeon than I thought possible, I didn't see her until she called out, "Stefan, over here!"

I carefully stepped around the other prisoners to reach her. I knew Puritans kept accused witches shackled, believing it would prevent them from changing into specters, but unlike the other women's shackles, only Tara's were chained to the wall. I stepped back out into the hallway, grabbed a musket, and returned to use it like a crowbar to pry the chain away from the wall.

I wasn't about to stay inside the dungeon to mess with Tara's shackles, however. Instead, I tossed Tara over my shoulder, carried her into the hallway, and began looking for the jailer's quarters. I located those quarters on the top floor, along with a ring of keys on a table. The smallest of the keys unlocked the shackles.

As soon as Tara was free, she declared, "We can't leave the women down there!"

"I don't intend to leave anyone behind," I said.

From the ring, I removed the key for the shackles and handed it to Tara. "Take this and release the women. I will take the rest of the keys and open the other jail cells."

In all, we released roughly thirty women—all from the same cell that Tara was in—and twenty men from five additional cells. Several of the women and a few of the men were in such terrible shape that we had to carry them out of the building. Others, presumably the more recently incarcerated, appeared to be in okay health.

Once we got everyone outside, the prisoners didn't disperse as we expected them to do. Instead, those who could stand just looked at us under the dim light of the cloudless night sky.

"Go! You are free!" I shouted from the front steps.

When they didn't move, Tara asked, "Do we just leave them here?"

"I don't think we have much choice."

The largest of the men we had released stepped forward—a shackle chain wrapped around his fist. "Are you ready for round three?" he said.

"No, Ralph!" I yelled. "These people are innocent."

"Then I guess you'll have to decide," he spat. "Either cripple them, like you did William Dounton and the others, or die!"

"Rodney!" I called out.

"Jackie Chan and Bruce Lee," he replied. "You are both good to go."

The man Ralph occupied swung his chain-wrapped fist! I ducked under and delivered a blow that dislocated his right shoulder. As he fell to the ground, screaming, another man came at me. I dislocated his shoulder too.

I glanced over at Tara, just in time to see her apply a kick to a man's testicles, sending him flying backward into the street.

"Be careful!" I shouted. "One of these men could be the great-great-grandfather of someone like Abraham Lincoln. If you make him sterile, you could damage history beyond repair!"

Another man came at me. This time he was ready for my move to dislocate his shoulder, and I had to take out his knee instead.

If the attacks weren't so heartbreaking, they would've been comical. I felt as if I were the hero in some cheesy martial arts flick. You know, the scene where the hero has to fight a group of villains, and the villains attack one at a time, instead of overwhelming the hero all at once.

Apparently, Ralph could only control multiple people in a near-simultaneous manner if they agreed with his goals. When they didn't agree, he could still control them, but he was limited to a more obvious one-at-a-time effort. Fortunately, Tara's and my refurbished skins were blocking Ralph from controlling us, or we'd be his puppets too.

Ralph's control limitations were especially noticeable around the edges of the crowd. Although some people were able to slip away, any man in good shape could only make it so far before abruptly turning and charging back into the fray.

"Tara! We need to go. Follow me!"

No matter how much control Ralph had over any body, he couldn't make it stronger or faster than it already was.

We disappeared into the forest, virtually unchallenged.

Chapter 32

The Cherry on Top

We were sitting on a fallen tree trunk, catching our breath, when Tara asked, "What do we do now?"

"Let's check in with our intergalactic handler." I looked up. "Rodney, what's our countdown to the time travel window?"

He materialized and said, "Thirty-three hours, nineteen minutes."

I perused Tara—her hair matted, her face and hands filthy—and said, "It's a warm night. Do you wanna go swimming?"

She beamed. "That would be heaven! Right now my skin feels like it's crawling, and I can't get the dungeon smell out of my nose."

"We can check out the river between Salem Village and Salem Town or we can find a lake."

"I prefer a lake," she said.

"GPS Rodney? Can you lead us to a lake in the woods?"

"The closest body of water that is also away from people is two miles from where you are now. It is more like a pond than a lake, but it should serve your needs."

Tara stood. "I'll race you there!"

Two miles isn't far when you are the fastest people on Earth. We ditched our clothes on shore and jumped in!

"Oh! It's cooo . . . ld!" screamed Tara. "And cold never felt so good."

We played in the water until we both felt refreshed, and Tara declared she could no longer smell the dungeon. After that, all that was left for us to do was pick up the high-tech camping gear I had buried, hide out at our campsite until the following night, and pay a final visit to Reverend Samuel Parris.

* * *

Even though we had given up hope of capturing Ralph on this mission, we had no doubt that Samuel Parris had been his enthusiastic partner in deceiving the people of Salem Village. And now that there was no need for deception, we simply waited until well after dark on July 18, kicked down the parsonage door, and used our enhanced eyesight to locate Ralph/Samuel. We pulled him out from under the covers, barricaded his wife and children in an upstairs room, and carried him to the church.

"You don't need to do this!" cried Ralph/Samuel. "I will leave on my own."

"And come right back after we depart," Tara said as she lit a lantern near the lectern.

Puritan churches didn't display crosses, so we had to make one out of some wood and some rope we found in an unfinished upstairs room. No. We didn't nail Ralph/Samuel to the cross. Our goal was to destroy his credibility, not physically hurt him.

Even so, I had to give Ralph some credit for staying inside Samuel's body as we pulled off his nightshirt, tied him to the cross, and hung the cross on the wall behind the lectern. Apparently, Ralph's curiosity was greater than his fear.

To complete the scene, Tara took some cold ash from the

woodstove and wrote "I love witches" across Ralph/Samuel's chest, using a heart symbol in place of the word *love*.

We stood back and admired our work.

"Not bad," I said.

"It's still missing something," Tara said with a smirk. She hurried from room to room, searching for supplies, before calling out, "I've got it!"

She returned with a broom and a piece of paper. She stared at the paper for a moment before announcing, "I was hoping to fold this into a witch's hat, but there isn't enough here to work with. It'll have to be a dunce's cap instead."

She slid the broom between Ralph/Samuel's legs and secured it with a piece of rope.

"Nice touch," said Ralph/Samuel with a slight smile. "But don't you think the cap will be excessive?"

"Oh, no," she replied. "It's the cherry on top!"

By this time, I was relaxed in a pew, watching, and feeling as amused by Tara's project as Ralph/Samuel now seemed to be.

Tara looked over her shoulder. "Honey, can you give me a boost? I'm not quite tall enough to put this cap on his head."

I walked over and clasped my hands into a stirrup. She stepped in, and I raised her up. She placed the cap atop Ralph/Samuel's head, pushed back a bit so she could make sure it was just so, and pulled herself closer to readjust.

"There," she said. "Perfect."

She thrust a trap-capsule into his ear! "Rodney now!"

Samuel went limp for a second before he stiffened and a terrified expression overtook his face.

As I lowered Tara, she threw her arms around my neck. "We got him! I know we did."

"Rodney?" I called.

He flashed in. "Hold on. I am checking." He flashed out.

While we waited, a quiet sniffle alerted us to look up at

Samuel. The reverend opened his mouth, as if trying to say something, but no words came out. He tried again, then dropped his head in frustration.

When Rodney reappeared, his somber expression told us all we needed to know.

The back door creaked open, and Samuel's daughter, Betty, stepped inside, shaking her head. *"Whew!* That was close! I must assume you're getting better at this."

The young body Ralph occupied marched over to the cross, turned to look up at Samuel and said to him, "I may be wicked, in a fun sort of way, but you are evil. Making your own daughter writhe in fits to further your influence was your idea, not mine." He stood on Betty's tiptoes and spit on him.

Ralph swiveled to look at Tara and me and grinned. "I guess this is goodbye for now. See you in Spain?" He raised the girl's hand and waved with just her fingers. "Toodle-oo!"

* * *

We left Betty with her father in the church. Her appearance meant that Samuel's family had breached our hastily stacked barricade, and someone would soon help Samuel down from the cross. With that in mind, we did the only thing we could do.

"Witch!" we screamed as we ran from house to house, waking people up. "A witch has been captured in the church!"

Soon people were lighting lanterns and streaming out of their houses.

Tara looked at me with a half-smile and said, "I think our work here is done!"

I glanced up. "Rodney, please guide us back to our campsite, and let us sleep until you can bring us home."

"I still have dibs on the first shower," Tara proclaimed.

Chapter 33

If at First You Don't Succeed

Tara and I returned home exhausted. Rodney must have felt the same way, or at least felt sorry for us, because he agreed to give us a three-day respite before our next time jump. That break would allow us to rejuvenate and think creatively about our last chance to save Planet Earth.

Tara did get the first shower, and she might have completely drained my well if she hadn't drained the hot water tank first. Later we enjoyed a candlelit meal, which included multiple courses and half of a banana cream pie each. The food tablets Rodney had provided us on our jump weren't as bland as you might have expected them to be, but they weren't crab legs dipped in butter, either.

Through all of this, Clarice was still clueless about our travels and apparently unconcerned that we kept popping out and back, smelling differently each time. Our being thrilled to see her after being gone for only an instant was cool with her too. Not letting her have a third of our banana cream pie was a different matter, however.

* * *

Our break from time traveling didn't mean a break from everything. The following day the three of us got together to discuss the destination for our final jump, and for that conversation, Tara and I sat on the couch and Rodney sat on his virtual chair.

"Obviously, this time we can't make any mistakes," I said. "And fortunately, we've learned quite a bit about Ralph. With that in mind, when, where, and in whom will we be most likely to find him?"

Rodney leaned back and said, "I have been spending a lot of time multitasking on the subject, and I have come up with three possibilities: your suggestion of Christopher Columbus, King Ferdinand II of Aragon, who began the Spanish Inquisition, and Durk the Terrible."

"Durk the Terrible?" Tara asked. "Don't you mean Ivan?"

"No. Durk is correct. He was quite likely one of Ralph's early attempts at using Christianity for revenge, but since Ralph had yet to become skilled at his pursuit, Durk never achieved much notoriety."

"He sounds perfect!" I said. "Incompetence is right up our alley."

Rodney raised a finger. "Not so fast. Durk lived in a walled city in what is now known as Romania. He may have been incompetent, but since he was royalty and constantly surrounded by guards, access to him would be nearly impossible. You would have difficulty getting through the gates without connections, and if you time traveled directly inside, you would have no place to hide and would likely be caught and executed as spies before the time travel window opened up."

"Wouldn't access be a similar problem with King Ferdinand?"

Tara asked. "I mean, we can't very well walk up to a king and say, 'Your Majesty, can we stick this up your nose?'"

"Yes, gaining access would be extremely complicated, and that is why I am leaning toward Christopher Columbus. There are multiple ways you can gain access to him. My main hesitancy is that there is only a 61 percent chance that Ralph is occupying Columbus as a primary subject. Sure, he fits the profile of an influential Christian who used his faith to justify repugnant behavior, but there were others during that time that fit that profile almost as well."

"Can we return to a time and place we've jumped to before?" I asked.

"Technically, there is no reason you cannot," Rodney said.

"What happens if we run into ourselves?" I asked.

"As long as the departure and return of your second jump is after the departure and return of your first jump—even by a second—you will be okay. That way you will have duplicates at your destination, but not when you return here to present time. I have to warn you, however, that meeting yourself will feel strange, and there is always the risk of getting into an argument with yourself over who is in charge."

I shrugged. "Strange, I can deal with, and the previous versions of us can suck it. The more experienced versions of us will know what we're doing."

"Where are you thinking?" Tara asked.

"I want to go back to Salem Village."

She tilted her head toward me and squinted. "Why?"

"Because I've considered every minute of our time there and have determined that one change will result in Ralph's capture."

"What change is that?"

"I'll show you. After all, our success will depend on you, and you're gonna have to practice over and over in front of Rodney and me until you can complete your task perfectly every time."

Chapter 34

Replay

T ara practiced her part for our final attempt to capture Ralph, and during breaks, we discussed whether creating duplicates of ourselves in present time would really be such a bad thing. We'd both seen movies on the subject, and in every one of them, having a duplicate led to disaster because one or more of the duplicates became dissatisfied with the working or romantic arrangements.

In our case, sharing the workload with a duplicate was appealing. Imagine only having to work every other week. Jealousy wouldn't be a concern either, since having equal duplicates would assure that no one was left out. And I suppose group sex might be something interesting to try too.

Nevertheless, the negatives of four people sharing the income of two, a cabin that was cozy for two being crowded for four, and the complications of always having to hide two of us from view confirmed that the movies were correct. Duplicates—at least in present time—were not a good idea.

That said, duplicating Clarice, so Tara and I could each have a warm dog on our lap, was a much better idea!

209

* * *

The following portion of our story includes two Taras and two Stefans. To minimize confusion, I will indicate the first versions of us with an *O* and an apostrophe. Depending on how you look at it, the *O* can stand for either *original* or a shout-out to the Irish.

* * *

Tara and I arrived in Massachusetts Bay Colony on July 16, 1692, a few minutes after our previous arrival. Since there was no need for us to hike through the forest again, Rodney had transported us directly to our pretty little campsite, next to the spring. By the time O'Tara and O'Stefan reached us, we had already set up our camp, leaving them the optimum spot on the moss to erect their tent.

O'Stefan saw us first. "Tara? Stefan? What are you . . . um, *we* doing here?"

"Don't tell me Fluffy is filling in for Rodney again!" O'Tara said.

"No, no, it's nothing like that," I said. "Tomorrow you two will have your best chance ever to catch Ralph. Unfortunately, you'll miss that opportunity, and he'll get away. We are six-day older versions of you who've returned because we know how to fix that error. And since we've already rehearsed what we need to do, you two can just kick back and enjoy your stay in 1692. The weather here is going to be beautiful!"

"That seems a little anticlimactic for me," O'Stefan said. "We must be able to help in some way."

"You can provide security outside the church," Tara said. "If our plan fails, a group of men with a gun will arrive, and I'll be thrown into the most disgusting jail imaginable. I just got the smell out of my nose and can't go through that again."

"And make sure you don't get killed," I added. "A weird aspect of time travel is that if one of you gets killed, your senior counterpart will poof into thin air. Conversely, we six-day-older versions are practically invincible. If one of us gets killed, Rodney will have you youngsters back to present time before you/we depart from the cabin a second time. Then you can either stop yourself/us from time traveling back to 1692 or tell yourself/us what happened, so you/we can avoid whatever caused that death."

O'Stefan closed his eyes and shook his head. "I think . . . that makes sense. . . . Okay, you just blew your own mind."

O'Tara smiled. "So if the bullets start flying, I'll hide behind Tara Senior."

O'Stefan chuckled and said, "Since you two have already experienced the coming days, how about filling us newbies in on everything?"

"I was just about to suggest that," I said.

The four of us found a comfortable spot to sit near the spring. There, Tara and I informed our duplicates of everything we had learned and our plan to do things better this time around.

Another mind-blowing aspect of time travel was that whatever O'Tara and O'Stefan were thinking or doing was immediately going into Tara's and my memories. In other words, our memories were being continuously altered. When I realized that was occurring, I wondered what would happen to our memories if our plan worked and we caught Ralph tomorrow and disappeared into the forest. We would have changed our own history. While I'm sure Tara wouldn't mind purging her memory of being thrown into the dungeon, and I know I wouldn't mind purging mine of all the people I had to maim, those events were part of us. Whether our memories would remain, like those we have of Donald Trump (a man who technically never existed), or melt away, was a mystery that only the passage of time could answer.

With that in mind, until the moment we hoped to capture

Ralph, we tried to do everything precisely as we had done the first time. Since there's no point in my repeating the details of taking to the forest like wild animals, our overnight stay, and our hike to Salem Village the following morning, let's jump ahead to when Tara and I stepped inside the church. The only difference this time is that O'Tara and O'Stefan are lingering outside and out of sight, ready to protect us if something goes wrong.

* * *

We opened the door to the church and stepped inside. Based on the body odor that assaulted us, I would have expected all the pews to be full. Instead, the only person inside was a slump-shouldered old woman sweeping the floor.

She looked at us and asked, "Are you seeking the Reverend Parris?"

"Yes," I said. "Do you know where we might find him?"

"He was here a moment ago. He probably went to fetch something at his parsonage. You can wait for him here if you like."

We sat in the nearest pew and looked around. The rectangular two-story building was as plain on the inside as it was on the outside. It had none of the stained glass windows, high ceilings, or crosses that you'd see in a modern church. Mostly, it was a dark, smelly, wooden box.

A few minutes later, a man who appeared to be about my age, with a hooked nose and brown, shoulder-length hair, entered through the rear door.

Tara and I stood.

"Reverend Parris?" I asked.

"Yes?"

"I'm Doctor Stefan Westin, from Boston, and this is my wife Tara."

He scowled. "Have you come to examine the afflicted? Or are

you just outsiders, coming to stick your noses into business that doesn't concern you?"

"May the love of Jesus bless you too!" Tara replied.

His face softened. "I'm sorry. Every time someone new arrives, I must assume Satan has sent him."

"Paranoid much?" she blurted.

Rodney materialized and shook a finger. "Sorry, I was not fast enough to mute you, Tara, but you are at least two hundred years too early to use that word." He disappeared.

She tried again. "You say *him*, but aren't most of the witches here women?"

His expression grew confused. "I don't see how the two are related. A minion from hell, sent by Satan, would take the form of a strong man. That's different from when Satan leads someone into witchery. Women are more sinful and weaker in the body and in the head than men are, and therefore easier for Satan to possess."

I put a hand on Tara's shoulder and whispered, "Let it go."

She brushed off my hand. "Sinful? It seems to me that the only one being sinful here is a *man* accusing multiple innocent women of witchery to raise his own status in the village."

Samuel trembled as he pointed a finger, inches from Tara's nose. "Witch!"

"I've been called a bitch before, but never a witch. Hmm . . . I kind of like it. But if you don't take that finger out of my face, this weak, sinful woman is gonna beat the living shit out of you."

He continued pointing as he screamed, "Witch! *Witch!*"

Tara's hand flashed faster than a viper strike. She grabbed Samuel by the wrist, twisted his arm behind him, and slammed his head to the floor as her free hand whooshed from the opposite side and jammed a trap-capsule into his ear! "Rodney, now!"

The slump-shouldered woman looked up from her sweeping and said, "Nice move, but no one here speaks like you do."

Tara reached down and pulled the trap-capsule from the dazed reverend's ear. "I knew I shouldn't have used the word *shit!*"

"No, shit is perfectly acceptable. You just can't wear the clothing of a weak Puritan woman and then come on strong."

Tara smiled and held out a hand. "How's it going, Ralph?"

He ignored her offer to shake. "Ralph? I hate that name! Call me Jesus."

"No. I like Ralph," she said.

He waved the slump-shouldered woman's hand dismissively and said, "It doesn't matter. Despite your obvious strength, it will do you little good when you're vastly outnumbered." Through the woman's eyes, he regarded the crumpled body on the floor. "I assume whatever you removed from his ear was designed to capture me."

"Yes."

"Can I see it?"

Tara held it up.

"Set it on the floor and smash it with your shoe."

She did as he said.

"I'm going to return to Samuel Parris now. This old body is full of aches and pains." The slump-shouldered woman sank into a pew. The reverend, apparently still dazed, did not move, however.

Tara and I looked at each other with wide eyes.

"Did he leave without saying 'toodle-oo'?" I asked.

"Apparently so."

"Well, you blew that one! You couldn't just ease into the mission? Get to know Samuel; gain his confidence; free some witches; that sort of thing."

"I'm sorry. He pissed me off."

The back door opened, and a dark-haired girl who appeared to be about ten stepped inside. She pointed a gun at us.

"A musket?" Tara asked. "No one told me there'd be guns."

"It's a Second Amendment model," I said.

"What?"

"The kind of gun the Founding Fathers had in mind when they wrote the Second Amendment."

"Yeah, I imagine it would be tough to shoot up a school with one of those."

"But it could kill one of us."

The girl aimed the gun at Tara before swinging it toward me. "Up against the wall!" she demanded in a mature voice.

She waited for us to follow her instructions. Then she handed the gun to Samuel Parris, who instantly recovered. The reverend stood and—

"Rodney, now!" Tara shouted.

Samuel collapsed on the floor.

Rodney flashed in and fist-pumped as he strutted from one side of our brains to the other. "We caught him!" He flashed out.

"Woo-hoo!" Tara and I shouted in unison.

O'Tara and O'Stefan raced in to exchange high fives with us.

Tara took a deep bow and declared, "Tara Kramer, magician extraordinaire! Ralph never even suspected I had two trap-capsules in my hand and left the first one in Samuel's ear."

"What a brilliant plan!" O'Stefan said as he shook my hand. "I couldn't have come up with a better one myself."

"All of you, hands up!" Samuel ordered.

The reverend had recovered during our celebration and was doing his best to point his musket at everyone at once.

Chapter 35

Ow!

We raised our hands.

"What did you do with Jesus?" Samuel asked.

"Do you mean Ralph?" O'Stefan replied.

"No, Jesus. He was in my heart, telling me what to do."

"I don't think that was his location in your body," O'Stefan said. "But no matter where he was, you're free to think for yourself now."

"I do not want to think for myself." He thrust his gun toward O'Stefan's chest. "Bring him back!"

O'Tara winced. "Which version of us can be shot, again? I forgot."

"I think it's us older ones," I said. "But before anyone risks taking a bullet, we should check with Rodney." I looked up and asked, "Rodney, what's your opinion on this?"

An image of Clarice appeared in our heads. "I am sorry," said the dog. "Rodney is unavailable. How may I help you?"

"Fluffy!" the four of us shouted in unison.

Samuel's face contorted with confusion. He waved his gun

back and forth as he screamed, "Witch! Witch! You are all witches!"

He pulled the trigger!

"Ow!" I screamed.

"Ow!" Tara screamed.

"Ow!" O'Stefan screamed.

"Ow!" O'Tara screamed.

We had all dropped to the floor, with our hands covering our ears. Enhanced hearing and an indoor gunshot are not a happy combination.

O'Stefan bolted from the floor, snatched the musket from Samuel, and smashed it over his leg. "Ow!" he screamed, louder this time.

"Ow!" I repeated, as pain began radiating from my femur. I glared at O'Stefan. "Did you really think you could bend an iron barrel?"

"I bent it a little. Now at least the gun won't shoot."

I stood and lowered my breeches. "Yeah, but look at my leg. Now I have a six-day-old bone bruise that I didn't have a minute ago. It hurts like hell."

"Mine hurts worse."

"I'm sure it does. And now my left arm hurts too." I reached with my right hand and felt a bandage. "Ah . . . my, *your*, arm is bleeding."

Both Taras sprang to their feet. O'Tara grabbed Samuel, so he couldn't get away, and Tara gently grasped O'Stefan's arm.

Fluffy frantically waved a paw. "Hey! Hey! I am still here. If you are going to ignore me, I will go away."

"Sorry about that, Fluffy," I said. "We no longer need an answer to our question and have things pretty much under control here."

"Hey, Fluffy," O'Tara said. "Is Rodney okay? He couldn't be due for another holy shit so soon."

She smiled (at least as much as a dog could smile). "Oh, he is doing great. He is handing over Ralph and probably getting a big promotion too."

"Good for Rodney," I said.

"So if you do not need me, I will turn off my visual image and continue monitoring until Rodney returns. If I do not speak with any of you again, congratulations on a fantastic job!"

"Thanks, Fluffy," O'Tara said.

She vanished.

"How's my arm?" O'Stefan asked.

Tara ripped a strip of cloth from the bottom of her skirt and tied it around his upper arm. "You were only grazed. I'll clean it up better and add a few stitches when we get back to camp."

"What do we do about Samuel?" O'Tara asked.

The experience of watching two sets of duplicate people, all talking to an invisible spirit named Fluffy, had the reverend quaking.

"I brought a proper witch's hat this time," Tara said. "We could string him up again."

"No," I said, looking around. "Betty and the old woman slipped out when we weren't paying attention. Others certainly heard the gunshot. The entire village will be here soon."

The sound of an approaching wagon filtered through the walls.

"And here they come," I said. "We have nothing to gain by hanging around and building up a body count."

"But what about the people in jail?" Tara asked.

I strode over to Samuel, grabbed him by mid-doublet, and lifted him above my head with one arm. "Listen carefully! The creature that was inside your body was not Jesus, and we have sent him to a place where he will never fool anyone ever again. The four of us have more power than that creature, or any witch, or any devil, or any god. You will immediately announce to the village and to the court that you were mistaken about the witches and that all who were arrested are innocent. You must not rest until everyone is released from jail. Do you understand?"

"Yes," he squeaked.

"Do you know what will happen if you disobey?"

"No."

I turned to O'Stefan and let him utter the words in a deep voice, "We'll be back!"

Still holding Samuel above my head, I carried him to the front of the church and deposited him atop the lectern.

The four of us slipped out the back as men burst through the front. We ran as fast as we could. For anyone rushing through the church and out the back door, we had created the illusion of disappearing into thin air.

We concluded our mission with a restful camping trip and a boisterous reunion with Rodney—full-time planetary consultant, first class.

Chapter 36

Toodle-oo!

Once back at the cabin, Rodney offered to give Tara and me a few quiet days to organize our thoughts. Even though we no longer had our duplicates, we still had near-duplicate memories of events from slightly different perspectives. For instance, for the same time I have a memory of lifting Samuel above my head, I also have my O'Stefan memory of watching me lift Samuel above my head.

Also, other than in pictures or contorting myself to look in a mirror, I had never seen the entire backside of my body before or noticed what I looked like when I walked. Those visions were kind of like when I was a kid and heard my recorded voice for the first time: not quite what I expected.

Strangest of all was that I could still remember breaking Tara out of jail. That, of course, really happened—until we changed history and it didn't happen. My best guess is that that memory is stored in my brain somewhat like a vivid dream. As time goes by, it will be interesting to see if that memory fades faster than those I have of other time jumps.

Although individually those phenomena may sound inconsequential, collectively they were a lot to deal with. I certainly wouldn't feel ready to do major surgery on anyone for a while.

Another concern of mine was how Tara and I would adjust to everyday life with powers that would remain extraordinary. It wasn't as if western Montana had much call for a side gig as the mysterious superhero Doctor Refurb. And besides, there might not be a single phone booth left in the state for me to use for changing into my tights.

I guess when I head back into the operating room, having stronger legs to stand on and better senses of sight and hearing might help me do my job better. As for Tara, she had already experienced the benefit of being able to run as fast as the dogs she works with.

Who knows? Perhaps someday the urge to display our powers will become irresistible. I could pursue my childhood dream of becoming a professional baseball pitcher, and Tara could smash a bunch of track and field records at the Olympics.

One thing was for sure: Tara and I would be together for the rest of our lives. We were heading toward marriage before Rodney popped into our heads, anyway. Now, after sharing so much, the thought of ever being apart was both inconceivable and impractical. Imagine how quickly some other lover would head for the door if I divulged to her, "My previous girlfriend and I saved the world through time travel and deporting environmental villains to a depository planet. I also have refurbished eyes, ears, arms, legs, and a liver that perform well beyond Earth-human specifications. Oh, and I should warn you before our relationship goes too far—my penis is refurbished too."

Tara would have similar difficulties—minus the penis thing. However, if she ever ended up with a lover or a husband who turned physically abusive, he would be in for one hell of a surprise!

Yes, we belonged together. In fact, you could say we were made for each other.

* * *

I assumed the next time Tara and I saw Rodney would be our last. While our relationship took time to grow, I think I will actually miss him. Sure, he withheld information from us, and every time I unzip my pants I will wonder where that penis came from. Nevertheless, I believe his heart was in the right place. (I say that metaphorically, because I don't know if he actually has a heart.)

Back at our campsite, near Salem Village, when we celebrated the capture of Ralph, Rodney hadn't mentioned any details resulting from our success beyond his promotion to full-time planetary consultant, first class, and his assurance that Earth wouldn't be recycled. Upon returning home, Tara and I did some checking on the internet and soon concluded that the world could wait a few more days while we processed everything we had been through.

Rodney must have been quietly observing us, because he didn't make another appearance until the two of us enjoyed a relatively normal day. We were relaxing on the couch, sipping hot chocolates and soaking up heat from the woodstove, when he materialized inside our heads.

"Knock! Knock! Good evening, my favorite Earth-humans. Is this a good time for a final get-together before I say goodbye?"

I waited for Tara to nod her approval before saying, "Your timing is perfect."

He eased into his virtual chair, dramatically cleared his throat, and began. "I ran multiple simulations, and when averaged together they predict that you have extended your planet's ability to sustain life by 193 years. That is less than the 200 my supervisor had required, but now that I am a full-time planetary consultant, first class, I was able to get Earth a Close Enough Waiver by arguing that the simulations cannot accurately account for the accomplishments of people who are now alive because of your efforts."

I stroked my chin, thinking back to a conversation that now seemed a lifetime ago. "Did you listen in on the conversation Tara and I had, when she suggested that among the lives saved by deporting Fred Trump could be a brilliant scientist or inventor who would come up with something to slow climate change significantly?"

"Yes. I think I have been clear about listening to all of your conversations, even if I was multitasking at the time. Now I can apologize for your lack of privacy, but monitoring your communications was one of my job requirements. My species values learning above all else, and learning about you two via recordings and my reports kept my supervisor and others in my department amused. That Tara so quickly grasped the concept of 'accomplishments by the now alive' certainly contributed to my supervisor viewing Earth-humans as slightly less inferior than she believed them to be. Ultimately, learning about instances like that made her more open to approving a Close Enough Waiver.

Tara rolled her eyes. "I'm tempted to make a snarky comment about how it was us *inferior* humans who outsmarted and caught one of your own, but since your supervisor agreed not to recycle Earth, I'll let it pass."

I tossed a log into the woodstove while I thought of questions to ask. If this was going to be our final conversation with Rodney, I didn't want to think of something the second after he poofed away. Eventually I said, "Tara and I haven't been ready to take a deep dive into the internet yet, but I did spend a short time looking around. One thing that struck me was that I didn't see a single story about COVID-19. I know changing history so Hillary Clinton became president instead of Donald Trump dramatically reduced COVID-19 cases, but it didn't eliminate them. Did something else happen that we hadn't anticipated?"

"I noticed that too," Rodney said. "Although I do not have a definitive answer, remember that you continued deporting people after Fred Trump. You also need to add to those deportations your elimination of Ralph's influence on the world beyond the year 1692. I do not know how many Christian politicians Ralph molded into anti-environmental politicians, but the number was significant, and his work on that spanned decades. Since climate change increases the risk of pandemics, that is one possibility.

"Another is that you now live in a friendlier world. A friendlier world means greater cooperation between countries and smaller military budgets that allow for more government funds to be allocated to science. While I have sophisticated simulation and prediction tools, those tools are still limited to observations and records they can access. They cannot, for instance, go inside people's minds, as I have done with yours, or see what happens behind closed doors at a biomedical research laboratory. Therefore, it is possible that COVID-19 was contained or wiped out before it even made the news."

He leaned forward. "There is one last possibility."

"What's that?" I asked.

"Some unintended change to the world that resulted from all the changes you have made. For instance, what if on the day the first person to catch the virus in the original timeline went elsewhere because of some event unique to the current timeline?"

"In other words," Tara added, "shit happens."

"Aside from my not having to treat COVID-19 patients when I go back to work, are there any other changes to Tara's and my personal lives that we should be aware of?"

"You have already experienced the next biggest change—your sister Amy being alive. As you figured out a long time ago, I have been able to protect your memories, so you could see your progress. Keep in mind that your two memories were the only protected ones. No one else will be aware of the changes. I also made sure you kept your careers and the cabin. And, as a special gift from me—not any timeline change—you will find your bank accounts a little heftier the next time you check them."

"Does the Republican Party still exist?" I asked.

"Yes, but with a big difference. In the original timeline, Republicans kept moving further to the right, while accusing the Democrats of being radical. That strategy was successful at moving the Democratic Party further to the right too. Now, in this new timeline, the pendulum has swung the other way, with the Republicans moving toward the middle and Democrats moving further to the left. That has resulted in enhanced environmental protections, universal healthcare, fewer military conflicts, safer and better-funded schools, less gun violence, more aid for the poor, increased trust in science, higher taxes on the rich, and expanded rights for women and minorities."

"Wow!" Tara said. "That's practically the entire liberal wish list."

"I imagine so," Rodney said. "But other than some whining from the ultra-rich, everything on the list benefits conservatives too. For instance, what person isn't better off breathing cleaner air and drinking cleaner water? The biggest reason for the change isn't a change of ideologies. It's that everyday Republicans no longer face a daily barrage of lies from Fox News and other far-right media to convince them to vote against themselves. Most liberal ideas are not radical—they are practical."

"What happened to Ralph?" I asked.

"He was convicted in a trial and will soon begin serving his punishment."

"What punishment is that?"

"As an advanced species, my people do not believe in a death penalty. Instead, we try to come up with unique ways to rehabilitate. After much deliberation, our highest court sentenced Ralph to fifty years in an inescapable, 100 percent refurbished, twenty-two-year-old human body."

I smiled nervously. "Yeah, I suppose it would be difficult living as a human among your people."

"Oh, no. That would not be possible. The only humane thing to do is send him back to Earth."

"Earth!" Tara screamed. "We just went through hell to get him off our planet!"

Rodney shook his head. "You will be fine. Ralph did most of his damage by switching from body to body and influencing people who were more primitive than now exist in present time. Those opportunities will no longer be available to him."

"But if he's in a 100 percent refurbished body, no one will be able to match his physical abilities, including Stefan and me."

"He'll have the missing ingredient—the equivalent of a bionic back," I added.

"I wouldn't worry about that," Rodney said. "An officer of the court will check in on Ralph every ten years to make sure he is on his best behavior, and he knows that if he stays out of trouble, he may qualify for an early release."

I swallowed the last of my hot chocolate before asking, "Can we lodge a protest with the court?"

Rodney's expression grew sympathetic. "I am sorry. Even as a full-time planetary consultant, first class, I am not authorized to question the court's decision."

Tara ran her fingers through her hair before asking, "If an officer is only gonna check in on Ralph every ten years, can you at least check in with Stefan and me more often? That way we can give you a first-hand report if he causes any trouble."

"All I can do is leave a special request with Fluffy to do so."

"Fluffy!" we blurted in unison.

"Yes, I am afraid your case has been handed over to her."

"Where are you going?" I asked.

"To observe the other half of this experiment," he said.

"What experiment is that?" Tara asked.

He shifted uncomfortably in his chair. "I am not supposed to tell you, but at this point I cannot see any harm in you knowing. In simplest terms, my people are planet farmers. We take uninhabited planets, optimize their surfaces and orbits as necessary, and give them life. Sometimes we provide early or follow-up guidance, as we did with your planet, but mostly we sit back and watch. Every planet provides us with exciting new knowledge that we use the next time as we endeavor to produce the perfect planet."

Tara narrowed her eyes. "Okay, so you're planet farmers. Considering everything we've experienced since meeting you, I don't find that surprising at all—or even something worthy of being secretive about. That doesn't explain what you mean by 'the other half of this experiment,' however."

Rodney stood. "My people created an identical planet on the far side of the galaxy and gave it identical early guidance. That planet has a Tara, a Stefan, a Donald Trump, a Samuel Parris, a Jesus, and even a rebellious Ralph. The humans there also call their planet *Earth*. Until the moment we met, there was no significant difference between the two Earths. When we realized that both planets were likely headed for failure, we decided to help one save itself. Yours was that lucky planet. My new assignment is to observe the probable death of that other Earth. When it is over, my people will take what we have learned from the diverging fates of the twin planets and add it to our quest for perfection."

"Thanks for choosing us." I looked down and shook my head. "I think."

"Yes. Thank you," Tara said.

"I know I have dropped a lot on both of you during our time together. I truly thank you for making my first experience as a

full-time planetary consultant a memorable one. Perhaps someday, I will find a way to pop into your heads for a reunion. Until
then, if you have no further questions, I will be on my way."

I held up a finger. "One last question."

"Go ahead."

"Would you have ever really wiped our memories?"

"No," he said with a smile. "A memory wipe would have been
too extreme for the transgression of quitting or being unable to
keep a secret. I apologize for misleading you about that, but it was
for your own good. Without such a threat, you would never have
cooperated. Also, the more people you talked to about what we
were doing, the greater the chance of your either being institu-
tionalized or persuaded not to participate. That said, I still recommend that you stay silent. No one, except possibly Amy, will
believe you anyway."

"I suppose you're right," I said.

Rodney folded his chair, tucked it under his arm, and turned
to walk away. "Toodle-oo!" he called out over his shoulder.

Author's Commentary

The Making of Doctor Refurb

When I write fiction, I insert as many true elements into my stories as I can. This novel required quite a bit of research to do that. Obviously, the politicians, pundits, and multimillionaires that Stefan, Tara, and Rodney fictitiously sent to the depository planet were real. While I do believe those environmental villains have had a substantial negative impact on our planet, I do not advocate their real-life deportation. Sometimes it's just fun to imagine it and wonder how much life on Earth would improve without them.

In the time travel adventures that took place in North America, Fred Phelps, Duncan Campbell Scott, and Samuel Parris were actual people, and I did my best to put them into fictitious situations that reflected the real-life impact on the people they hurt.

In the time travel adventures that took place in Brazil and Italy, I made up Reverend Wesley Wilson, the well-dressed priest, and the Saint Zoticus Catholic School for the Deaf. Although I can't say for sure that there was a missionary in Brazil who went as far as to declare himself Jesus's only male cousin, or a Catholic school for the deaf with a torture chamber in the basement, inspiration for those stories came from real reports of child abuse committed by missionaries in South America and priests at a Catholic school for the deaf in Italy.

For readers who think I went too far with my depictions of child abuse by Christian authorities, the real-life child abuse I found in my research often made my fictitious depictions of such abuse pale in comparison. Holding back was a conscious decision on my part, because including too much graphic realism would have made this novel too depressing to read.

If there is a god who watches over our planet, I think we all need to ask him/her, "How can you stand by while authorities representing virtually all religious denominations commit such hideous crimes?" And when that god proves unable to answer our question, we must approach the problem more realistically and ask our political leaders, "How can our government stand by and do so little?" While some religious authorities are being charged for their crimes, countless others escape punishment. Any nonreligious organization committing even a fraction of the child molestations committed by religious organizations would not be allowed to exist.

If you are a Christian and you read all the way to the end of this novel, congratulations on maintaining an open mind! At the same time, I know some Christian readers are fuming at me, eager to post one-star reviews on various book sites. For those people, I ask that they remember that I was careful to separate the two dominant factions of Christians. I never said "all Christians," as this book is aimed only at those Christians who use their religion as a weapon to acquire sexual gratification, money, fame, control, or power.

Thank you for reading this. And if I made you laugh or smile, please post a review on your favorite book site and read my other books. Whether I'm writing fiction or nonfiction, all of my books use humor to promote peace, compassion, nondiscrimination, and the preservation of our planet for future generations.

Finally, I wrote *Doctor Refurb* to be a stand-alone novel, but as I neared the end, I decided to leave open the possibility for another Stefan, Tara, and Rodney adventure. If that happens, you can expect to see it a year or two after the publication of this book.

Cheers!

Please Review This Book

Reviews are important! If you enjoyed *Doctor Refurb*, please post a review on the website of the retailer where you purchased this book. Stefan Westin and Tara Kramer thank you in advance for any review you post, and Rodney guarantees that posters of five-star reviews will never be deported to a depository planet.

About the Author

The author before going on stage at Eastern Arizona College

Marty Essen grew up in Minnesota and resides in Montana. In addition to being an author, he is also a talent agent and a college speaker. Since 2007, Marty has been performing *Around the World in 90 Minutes* on college campuses from coast to coast. *Around the World in 90 Minutes* is based on his first book, *Cool Creatures, Hot Planet: Exploring the Seven Continents,* and it has become one of the most popular slide shows of all time.

Please enjoy all of Marty Essen's books:

Cool Creatures, Hot Planet: Exploring the Seven Continents
Winner of six national awards. Features 86 photographs.

Endangered Edens: Exploring the Arctic National Wildlife Refuge, Costa Rica, the Everglades, and Puerto Rico.
Winner of four national awards. Features 180 photographs.

Time Is Irreverent
If you enjoyed *Doctor Refurb*, you will love the entire *Time Is Irreverent* series!

Time Is Irreverent 2: Jesus Christ, Not Again!

Time Is Irreverent 3: Gone for 16 Seconds

Time Is Irreverent: Ooh, It's a Trilogy! (Books 1-3)

Hits, Heathens, and Hippos: Stories from an Agent, Activist, and Adventurer
A humorous memoir, with rock 'n' roll, headhunters, a demon-possessed watch, and a hippo attack.

For information on Marty Essen's speaking engagements and for signed copies of his books, please visit www.MartyEssen.com. For beautiful nature photography and biting political commentary, please visit www.Marty-Essen.com.

Readers are welcome to write the author at Marty@Marty-Essen.com or to send him a Facebook friend request at www.facebook.com/marty.essen.